NIGHT AT CASTLE MORVANT

I slipped from bed and moved cautiously to the door. Directly across the hall, the door to Amorita's room was open. I stepped into the hall and saw a figure coming up the stairs. I stood motionless, but enough moonlight slipped through a window at the end of the hall to reveal my presence.

As the person came nearer, I saw that it was a woman... Amorita. I spoke her name; she wheeled around. In her hand I could see the silhouette of a revolver. It was pointed directly at me.

Warner Books
by Dorothy Daniels

THE BEAUMONT TRADITION
THE CALDWELL SHADOW
HILLS OF FIRE
JADE GREEN
THE LARRABEE HEIRESS
A MIRROR OF SHADOWS
THE TORMENTED
THE APOLLO FOUNTAIN
DARK ISLAND
DIABLO MANOR
THE DUNCAN DYNASTY
THE HOUSE OF BROKEN DOLLS
THE HOUSE OF MANY DOORS
THE LANIER RIDDLE
THE MARBLE HILLS
SHADOWS FROM THE PAST
THE SUMMER HOUSE
PERRINE
CONOVER'S FOLLY
THE SILENT HALLS OF ASHENDEN

**ARE THERE WARNER BOOKS
YOU WANT BUT CANNOT FIND IN YOUR LOCAL STORES?**

You can get any Warner Books title in print. Simply send title and retail price, plus 50¢ to cover mailing and handling costs for each book desired. New York State residents add applicable sales tax. Enclose check or money order only, no cash please, to:

WARNER BOOKS
P.O. BOX 690
NEW YORK, N.Y. 10019

CASTLE MORVANT

Dorothy Daniels

WARNER BOOKS

A Warner Communications Company

WARNER BOOKS EDITION

Copyright © 1972 by Dorothy Daniels
All rights reserved

Library of Congress Catalog Card Number: 79-187690

ISBN 0-446-84828-X

Cover art by Norman Walker

Warner Books, Inc., 75 Rockefeller Plaza, New York, N.Y. 10019

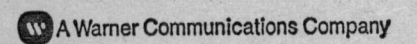

A Warner Communications Company

Printed in the United States of America

Not associated with Warner Press, Inc. of Anderson, Indiana

First Printing: March, 1972

Reissued: August, 1978

10 9 8 7 6 5 4 3

ONE

All through this vast darkness, there was the subtle odor of decay. The slow, sinister music of the ancient and battered piano seemed muffled by the lack of proper acoustics. I sat on a high-backed, carved chair, cushioned in bright red velvet. From the surrounding gloom, the ghost appeared.

At first he was a swirling shadow, all in white, and then, as the lighting improved, he began moving slowly toward me. I sat, rigid with fear, until he was directly before me. I arose slowly, extended my hand toward him and he backed away with a series of small, stylized steps.

From out of the shadows beyond him came another ghost, a girl, young and lovely, moving gracefully toward him, en pointe, extending her hand as I was extending mine. I wished to lure him from the land of the dead; the ghost wished him to remain. The young man, torn between the two, paused, confused and uncertain.

That was the theme of the *Ballad of Lorraine*. It was I who spoiled the so-far perfect illusion by tripping over a bit of loose board. I'd known it was there, but in my anxiety for perfection I forgot, and the entire sequence of my dance was lost. I cried out involuntarily as I was thrown off balance.

Mirabel Rousseau called out for lights and the dimmed stage brightened. I looked out into the darkened casino for a glimpse of her. She and Theodoric Coubet had been seated at one of the tables still assembled in a part of the room where a drinking and dining audience once sat. The remainder of the corps de ballet, concealed in the wings, came out and gathered around. They knew rehearsal would be suspended for the day.

Mirabel and Theodoric left their chairs and came on stage. The latter began a careful inspection of the stage floor, beginning with the board which had tripped me.

Mirabel said, "Are you hurt, my dear?"

"No," I replied. "Just annoyed I could have been so careless. I noticed that loose board when we started to rehearse."

"You should have told me about it." Her voice was gently chiding. "Neither Theodoric nor I would have allowed a rehearsal had we known."

Theodoric spoke from the far side of the stage. "I found two more. I'll have them repaired immediately."

"Please do," Mirabel urged. "We have only one month to rehearse. Our first day hasn't started very auspiciously."

Theodoric attempted to placate her. "Please don't begin worrying. We'll use the time to further acquaint the cast with the story of the *Ballad of Lorraine*. And this time I'll go into more detail."

"But not too long, Theodoric," Mirabel said plaintively. "The stage must be repaired."

"It will be, my dear," he replied patiently. "It will be."

Theodoric Coubet was dignified, white-haired, with

the broad shoulders and slender figure of a man many years his junior. He was once a famous danseur noble with the Paris Ballet. One of the young male dancers ran to an ancient piano and returned with a round stool, placing it for Mr. Coubet. He nodded his thanks, took a thin cigar from his pocket, and held it in the manner of a baton. All of us, without being told, sat in a semicircle around him, being careful to avoid the broken board.

He regarded us a moment before speaking, to make certain he had our attention. "Now, my pets, let me apologize first of all, for being forced to have you rehearse in this cold, run-down, abandoned building which was once a gambling hall-night club. But I had no choice. We do wish to get this ballet ready to open the season in November, do we not, my pets?"

There was a chorus of agreements, though I detected a few smirks at his term of endearment. They well knew Mr. Coubet could be a martinet when it came to perfection of performance from each member of the ballet, no matter how minor the role.

Mr. Coubet went on, "I only hope the beauty of the Lake Tahoe area will recompense you for the long journey here. Perhaps some of you still don't know that it was made necessary because Oriano, our premier danseur, has a contract at the biggest of the gambling palaces as star of their very fine review. And since we want Oriano—and he is willing to rehearse with us even while working—we have come to him."

Oriano bowed respectfully. "Thank you, Theodoric. And the rest of you, also. And in appreciaton, I hope all of you will be my guests tonight at the casino."

Mr. Coubet looked pleased. "A most gracious gesture."

The cast applauded; Oriano blew them a kiss.

Holly Larkin, who was the ghostly presence endeavoring to keep Oriano from leaving the world of the dead to enter my world, which was that of the medium, spoke. "I'm delighted that we had to come here. It will really be a vacation."

"It will be no such thing, Holly. And you'd better remember it." Sternness crept into Mr. Coubet's voice. "I will rehearse you twenty hours a day if need be. Now, to business. What I wish to talk to you about is the theme—or the plot—of this ballet. It is based upon fact. What we will portray actually happened, and not long ago. But let Mirabel tell you. She has done the book."

Mirabel Rousseau was not a dancer, but a woman who loved ballet. As she could be no part of the dancing, she contented herself with writing ballets, sometimes helping with the score, more often supervising the business end of the production. She was about forty, I judged. A handsome woman with strong features, and growing just a bit broad around the hips. Something she blamed on the fact that she spent so much of her time sitting at a desk. Which was probably true. I'd known her for two years and was impressed with her dedication to ballet.

"All right, kids," she said. "Theo is correct—this did happen. In a town where I lived at the time. That's how I got the idea. Lorraine was a medium, just as she is in the ballet. Actually, she was an out-and-out fake. All of them are, but she could put on a very good act. So clever, in fact, that I attended several of her seances before I was convinced it was all a hoax."

"And did she actually fall in love with a ghost?" I asked.

"That's what she claimed. Anyway, you must admit it makes a good idea for a ballet."

"It's certainly working out well the way you've written it, Mirabel," I said.

"Thanks, Nicolette. Well, Lorraine had conjured up the ghost of this handsome young man. Not just his voice, but the manifestation of his body. He was there, in person. Or rather, his ghostly presence was there."

Some of the cast had arrived late and were not completely familiar with the story. Mirabel looked pleased by their rapt attention, knowing they were already intrigued with the little they'd heard.

"She promptly fell in love with him, but it seems that the young man had a romance in his world of ghosts, with a very beautiful ghost who loved him . . . that's you, Holly."

"Lucky me," Holly Larkin said, and her eyes shifted to Oriano, who regarded her with interest.

Mirabel continued, "Now the ghost of the young man found himself torn between the human medium and his ghostly girl friend. This is going to be most effective, the way Theo has choreographed it."

"What really did happen?" I asked Mirabel. "I mean, in that town where Lorraine was murdered."

"No one knows for sure. In my book for the ballet, the ghost of the girl kills Lorraine, out of desperation and fear that Lorraine somehow might turn the ghostly young man into a human. She warns Lorraine several times by creating accidents that come close to killing the medium. When that doesn't work, she finally does kill her. It is an established fact that the real Lorraine did suffer several accidents."

"I meant to ask this," Theo said. "Was there a murder?"

Mirabel gave a nod of her head. "It was a homicide. One that has never been solved."

"How," Holly asked, "did this ghost, whose part I take, kill Lorraine?"

"By fire," Mirabel said quietly.

I said, "The way you've brought it out in the ballet removes all the horror of what you've just told us. You've made it a gentle love story. Even those attempts of the girl ghost to warn Lorraine are never bloodcurdling."

"If they were, it wouldn't be ballet," Mirabel said. "In real life, though, the attempts on Lorraine's life must have been terribly frightening to her."

"Why did she continue to have seances and seek out the ghost, when she'd met with so many accidents?" I asked.

"She probably didn't associate them with the girl ghost," Holly suggested.

"Oh yes, she did," Mirabel countered.

"Then it turned into a battle of wits between Lorraine and the girl ghost," I suggested.

Mirabel said, "Probably that was it, since Lorraine persisted in having seances and bringing the young man back. And each time he returned, so did his ghostly girl friend."

"What a delightful role I have," Holly exclaimed. "I can be beautifully wicked and I shall enjoy every moment."

Mirabel smiled tolerantly. Holly's ego was no secret, but she always gave a fantastic performance, so we overlooked her constant references to herself.

Mirabel said, "Lorraine stated that the girl ghost was the spirit of a ballet dancer—a prima ballerina—in life. Lorraine swore she recognized her when she materialized."

"Oh, come on," Holly scoffed.

"I'm serious," Mirabel said. "Did you ever hear of Katiana?"

"One of the greatest dancers in the Russian ballet," I said.

Mirabel nodded. "So you see, Holly, you must give the performance of your life."

"As a ghost," Holly quipped. "I'm not familiar with Katiana."

Oriano walked over to her side. His dark eyes looked searchingly into her blue ones and a smile touched one corner of his mouth. "You haven't done your homework, beautiful."

"I shall make it a point to find out all I can about her," Holly said, color flushing her cheeks at his attention.

"I shall make it a point to inform you about her this evening," he replied. He reached for her hand, bent forward and kissed it.

If it had been anyone else, a reprimand would have promptly come from Theodoric, but no one reprimanded Oriano. His talent was exceeded only by his temperament, and he was in such great demand and commanded such a high salary, that his little vagaries were overlooked—for when he was on stage, he was music and poetry in motion.

Mirabel looked rather amused. "I think," she said, "you will both perform beautifully together."

"Be assured of it," Oriano replied, never taking his eyes from Holly.

It was understandable. Her blonde beauty was ethereal; her figure, slender, graceful, and enticing. She took a few backward steps, as if only by widening the distance between herself and Oriano could she regain her senses.

She spoke softly and the tremor in her voice gave evidence of the effect he had on her. "I'm sure I'll be as ethereal as ectoplasm in the role of Katiana. I may even vanish."

"If you do, my lovely one, I shall vanish with you," Oriano said, without a hint of a smile, giving one the feeling that he could do it. He was a superb actor as well as a dancer, for even his voice was a caress. Or was it that I was envious? I hoped not. I felt no quickening heartbeat as I regarded him, though I'd not deny he was handsome, with a superb physique. Yet I couldn't believe in his genuineness. I had danced with him before, and had watched him use the adoring eyes, slow smile and hand-kissing on many girls.

"And spoil my ballet?" Mirabel asked in mock dismay.

Theodoric looked up at her. "It appears you will have a pas de deux beyond your greatest expectations."

"I'm sure of it," she said.

Theodoric turned his attention back to the cast. "I believe everyone understands the ballad now. Tomorrow we start rehearsals. Be here at nine, please. Thank you. Now run along and have your fun. After today, you'll have little time for it."

The girls ran backstage to slip on skirts or slacks over their leotards; the boys hadn't donned rehearsal clothes, so they needed only to change from dancing slippers to street shoes. They reappeared minutes later, chattering animatedly and calling out their good-byes.

Holly and I shared a dressing room. I started backstage and, to my surprise, was joined by her. She said, "I'm to be Oriano's special guest tonight at the casino."

"Wonderful," I said, returning her smile. She looked radiant.

"Will you be there?" she asked.

"No," I replied. "I'm going to turn in early. You know how Theodoric will drive us once rehearsals begin. I don't want to start tired."

"You're right, of course," she said. "But I'll certainly not turn down a date with Oriano."

"What girl would?" I replied. "But I'll content myself with dancing with him."

We reached our dressing room and I buttoned a yellow skirt over my black leotard. I had a wide woolen stole in a matching color and I draped it over my shoulders, for there was a decided chill in the air and I couldn't risk catching cold. A ballerina with a cold is about as useful in her work as a pediatrician with the measles.

Holly donned a short red wool jumpsuit over her leotard, then pulled on matching suede boots which covered her knees. The effect was striking and I told her how stunning she looked.

"Thanks," she said. "How do you like the story of the *Ballad of Lorraine?*"

"Fantastic. I think it's quite likely to be among the

great contemporary ballets, like DeMille's *Fall River Legend*."

"I agree, though I was reluctant to take the part."

"Why?"

She wrinkled her nose. "Coming all the way across the country, when conditions for our work would be so much better in New York. Back there, as the prima ballerina, you'd even have your own dressing room."

"I'm glad to share this one with you," I said.

"For a moment today, I thought I was going to move into your role."

Startled, I paused in the act of powdering my nose. "Oh," I shrugged off her remark. "The loose board."

"Better luck next time," she quipped.

"You or me?" I asked, regarding her reflection in the table mirror.

She slipped her shoulder-strap bag over her arm and headed for the door. "Me, of course. I'd be a liar and a hypocrite if I pretended I didn't want the role of prima ballerina—any way I could get it."

"That's pretty brutal," I exclaimed.

"It's honest. Maybe you'll break an arm on the slots."

"I don't gamble," I retorted.

"A pity," she said and was through the door. She didn't bother to close it, and I sat there until her brisk footsteps faded and nothing remained but the quiet of the empty theater.

Though I'd never worked with Holly before, I knew her reputation as an opportunist. She seemed to like the idea of becoming prima ballerina by clawing her way to the top, yet her talent was such that she couldn't help but make it on that alone. I recalled gossip that she seemed bent on feuding with someone in whatever ballet she played. Apparently, I was the target for this one— and I didn't like it. I could stand up to her, but I wanted no rivalry on stage. Only the days ahead would reveal if I'd be successful in avoiding it.

I thought of what a good foil we were for one another. She with her blonde beauty, and I with my jet black hair center-parted and coiled atop my head. I was not as tall as Holly, and while I could never be termed beautiful, as Holly was, I was small-boned, with oval features, in contrast to her round face. Yes, we were distinct opposites, which was good, not only for the roles we played, but for the fact that the contrast made us immediately identifiable by the audience.

TWO

When I returned to the stage, everyone had gone. A single naked bulb had been left burning, but it didn't illuminate much beyond the footlights. I was facing an empty cabaret, dark as night, and for some reason I felt a tremor of fear, as if something waited for me out there in the gloom.

I quickly threw off the feeling of apprehension, attributing it to my brief exchange with Holly, and went over to the ornate chair, the prop which I would use in the show when I was holding a seance. I hadn't felt comfortable in it and it seemed more a hindrance than a help. I had to be able to rise from the chair with the utmost grace, and go into my dance without altering any body movements or missing a beat of the music.

I sat down and discovered why I couldn't get out of it gracefully. Like many ballerinas, I was not tall and my feet didn't quite touch the floor when my spine was against the back of the chair. I could compensate for that by having a pillow made of the same color as the upholstery. I would speak to Mirabel about it.

Something clattered against the floor almost at my feet, distracting me. I saw a dull, reddish object, and I was curious enough to rise and pick it up. I was holding a large, rusted nail which had apparently fallen from the rafters above. I looked up. Something was swinging far above my head. I knew what it was—a sandbag. A counterweight to the main curtain. This ancient theater-restaurant would have those, of course.

I flung myself out of the chair and ran to the far end of the stage. The sandbag came crashing down onto the red velvet chair with such force that all four legs snapped off. I stared at the wreckage for a long moment, trembling with a fear that wouldn't be stilled. I knew it was an accident, yet panic overwhelmed me. I wanted to get out of here as fast as my feet could carry me.

I ran down the stage steps, along the aisle, and paused only when I reached the lobby. I stopped not because I wanted to, but because my way was blocked by a gentleman at least six feet two. He was wearing white duck trousers and a white sport shirt. He had black hair styled close to his head, and he was clean-shaven. Certainly his appearance shouldn't have instilled further fear in me, but I cried out at the sight of him.

His pleasant features assumed a look of concern and he reached out to grip my arms, but I stepped back, evading any contact with him.

"What happened, Miss Artaude?"

"How do you know anything happened?" I retorted, still annoyed at his having blocked my path.

"You look as if you had a fright or a shock of some kind." He paused, then added, "Or is it just that the rehearsal went badly?"

"Nothing like that," I began, then said, "Yes, the rehearsal did go badly and I just had a fright."

"What sort of fright?" he asked.

I managed a smile, feeling suddenly embarrassed at my cowardice. "A sandbag fell and almost landed on me."

"You've every right to be frightened," he said. "I'm Steve Fenmore, by the way, an M.D. How did it happen?"

"I was sitting beneath it, but thanks to a rusty nail which fell first, I looked up, saw it swinging, and knew it was going to fall."

He looked puzzled. "That's odd. My aunt—actually she's my grandaunt—owns this building. She had the stage, the catwalk and, I'm sure, the sandbag weights all inspected before you came up here."

"Is that how you know my name?" I asked.

He smiled. "No. I've seen you perform several times."

I was intrigued. He didn't seem the type who'd go for ballet. "You like ballet?"

"Not too much," he admitted. "But my aunt dotes on it. She particularly admires you and wishes to meet you. That's why I'm here."

"That's very kind of her. Is she outside?"

"No. I was hoping you'd let me drive you over to her place. But after the fright you've had, I can understand your refusing. I'll take you back to where you're staying. First though, if you don't mind, I'd like to see that sandbag."

"You do believe me, don't you?"

"Of course. But when I tell my aunt what happened, she'll blow up. Someone was careless. She even had every board of the stage inspected. I know. She insisted I bring her here while it was being done."

"Are you sure?" I asked.

He noted my skepticism. "Positive. I had a heavy schedule that day and I had to crowd it in order to bring her here. Why do you question it?"

"Because I almost took a header on a loose board. It broke up the rehearsal."

17

"So that's why everyone left so early. I happened to have a free afternoon and I was waiting outside for you. Having seen you perform, I knew I'd have no difficulty recognizing you, but when you didn't come out, I decided to come in—at a most inauspicious time. I scared you half to death."

I finally managed a smile. "Only because of the fright I'd already received. I'm ashamed of myself for running out of here."

"I'll take you to my car and then I'll come back here and check the fallen sandbag. I also want to see the loose floorboard."

"Mr. Coubet found two more."

"I'm afraid the inspection wasn't very thorough," Dr. Fenmore said. "My aunt's not going to like that. She was delighted when her rental agent informed her that Miss Rousseau had contacted him regarding the leasing of the cabaret."

"I take it your aunt is a true ballet fan," I said as we moved briskly down the aisle to the stage.

"I don't know if her name would mean anything to you—Amorita Davina?"

"The great Davina is—here at Tahoe?" I had stopped myself barely in time from asking incredulously if she was still alive. Amorita Davina was a legend, not a person.

"Yes. She has a house near Incline Village. An old, enormous place that looks as if it must be haunted, but she loves it there. When she bought it, it was called Castle Morvant. She liked the name and kept it. It resembles a castle, and she fell for it since she used to be a castle buff and traveled all over Europe inspecting them."

Dr. Fenmore stepped back to allow me to climb the steps. He followed and whistled softly as he noted the sandbag atop the smashed chair.

"I don't wonder you got such a fright."

"I don't think it was altogether because of the sandbag falling."

"What do you mean?" He bent down and picked up the piece of rope attached to the sandbag.

I was thinking of Holly's parting taunt. Yet it would be unfair to repeat what she'd said. She wouldn't be the first who'd wished the lead in a show would meet with some kind of accident so that she might take her place.

I said, "I was sitting in the chair, thinking about the ballet we're going to rehearse. It's a spooky sort of thing and the combination of the empty cabaret, the gloominess of the unlit interior, along with the idea of a ghost killing a human, was too much for me, especially once the sandbag came down. I'm just grateful for the rusty nail which preceded its fall."

"So am I." He was regarding the end of the rope. "Particularly since this rope was cut. This was not an accident."

I went over and looked at the rope. There were no frayed or rotten strands. The rope appeared to be in good condition, but it had been cut, all except one little section which couldn't possibly have supported the heavy weight.

He said, "Where are the loose boards?"

I pointed with my toe to the one I'd tripped on, then moved to the other side of the stage where Theodoric had discovered the other two.

"Can you think of anyone who'd do such a thing?" he asked.

"No," I replied. "Can you?"

He regarded me curiously. "If you're asking if my aunt has any enemies in these parts, it's possible. She's high-spirited, strong-willed, and outspoken."

"I'd like to meet her," I said. How old must she be, I wondered, trying to remember my ballet history. In her seventies, I guessed.

He looked hopeful. "Now?"

"Now," I replied. "I'm over my fright, though I don't like the idea of the rope having been deliberately cut."

"Nor I," he said. "I wonder if someone is out to make trouble for my aunt."

"Someone in particular?" I asked.

He looked thoughtful. "There's a combine that wishes to buy out a large section of property around here, including this building. She owns most of it. The two other owners are willing to sell. She refuses, even though the combine upped its price twice."

"And you think this may be a way of getting your aunt to have second thoughts about not selling?"

"Possibly, though the combine seems quite reputable." He regarded me with concern. "I'm going to have to tell my aunt about this."

"At her age, do you think you should worry her?"

He looked amused. "Come along. Meet her."

His car was parked just beyond the entrance. It was a white sports car, an expensive one. The area around the cabaret was devoid of any signs of life, being an isolated part of the lakefront, just south of Emerald Bay. Once this had been a busy area, but it had died and the cabaret had died with it, when the new, ornate casinos, hotels, and motels had been built at the very edge of the lake.

"Whatever made you come all the way to Tahoe to rehearse a ballet which will be performed in New York?" he asked.

"Oriano, our leading male dancer, is under contract to a casino here. He agreed to accept the part with us, though, provided we came here to rehearse. With Oriano, we're assured of a full house."

Dr. Fenmore gave me a chiding look. "Since when have *you* played to empty seats?"

I smiled, thanking him with my eyes. "Nonetheless, I'm very pleased to have Oriano as a partner. He's superb."

"I agree. I've seen him. Suppose we have a cocktail before I take you to my aunt's."

"I'd like a glass of sherry. It will relax me."

"Good." He opened the low door for me and I settled myself into the deeply padded cushions. I had to refrain from smiling as I watched him ease his six feet two behind the wheel and settle down. He turned the key in the ignition and the motor purred into life. He backed the car skillfully between full-grown pines until he faced the road, then shifted, and we moved onto the narrow, two-lane highway. It was a short drive to one of the casinos and we went into the cocktail lounge.

Dr. Fenmore guided me to a table, then excused himself to check with his office, asking me to order. Unlike most cocktail lounges which had muted lighting and soft music, lending an air of intimacy, this one was well-lit, with a room temperature no higher than sixty degrees. The reason for this wasn't difficult to analyze. One wouldn't linger here for any length of time. The constant clatter of the slot machines drifted through the wide opening, a reminder that the action was beyond this room, though a girl paused at our table, selling cards for Keno, which was going on constantly. A boxed board was attached to the walls facing the tables, lighting the numbers which came up. I declined and the girl moved on.

Dr. Fenmore returned, told me he was free, and immediately turned the conversation to what had happened at the cabaret.

"Can you imagine anyone who'd want to harm you?"

"Not really, Doctor."

"What do you mean—not really?"

I shrugged. "I can't imagine anyone wanting to kill me. Perhaps a sprained ankle or back—something that might force me to leave the show."

"And who'd want that?"

I smiled. "I'm not sure anyone would. However, Holly

Larkin has an important role. And after I tripped on the loose board, she mentioned that for a little while she'd thought she was going to move into my part. Then she added, 'Better luck next time.'"

"She sounds sweet."

"I'm sure she didn't mean it. She's convinced that the ballet world is cutthroat; one has to be an opportunist."

"But not a murderer—or murderess."

"I'd swear she had nothing to do with cutting that rope."

"Nonetheless, I'm going to report it to the police."

"Oh, please don't," I exclaimed. "I don't want any adverse publicity for the ballet. After all, I wasn't injured."

"You could have been killed," he said sternly, "and it should be reported. The place has been empty for years. Some drifter or dropout could even be using it as a refuge, and could resent the fact that you and your company took it over, dispossessing him. He could've cut the rope, hoping to frighten you away."

"Since it didn't work, he'll not try it again, I'm sure."

"He might try something else. Don't forget the loose boards."

"You don't know if they were deliberately loosened."

"No," he admitted. "But it seems likely they were."

"Please don't report this," I begged. "I don't want Mirabel or Theodoric upset. This is Mirabel's big chance. She's done other ballets, but this one, I'm certain, will really make her reputation."

He smiled at my earnestness. "Very well. But I must tell my aunt about it. And if anything further happens, promise you'll contact me immediately."

"I promise, Doctor."

"Make it Steve, will you, please?"

"Steve. I'm Nicki."

"I like it. Now, suppose we visit my aunt. I'll take you there on the road that skirts the lake."

"The lake is fantastic. Just how big is it?"

"Twenty-two miles long and twelve miles wide. It's a shame the area has been so commercialized by the casinos. Of course, they're only on the Nevada side. The California side will have no part of it. But we have the Sierras on both sides, adding to the beauty, and the forests are national preserves. So it could be worse."

"The air is so clean," I exclaimed. "My lungs still haven't got over the shock of it."

"Where is your home?" he asked.

"An apartment in New York City. My parents are dead and I live alone."

"I can understand why you appreciate the fresh air here."

I was pleased to leave the cold room and be once again warmed by the late afternoon sun. We drove for a while in silence, admiring the beauty of the lake and the surrounding countryside. We reached a picnic area where several long tables were placed, along with small brick fireplaces for the convenience of picnickers. A section had been marked off for parking and it fronted the lake. Steve moved into a slot, killed the motor, and settled back.

"I'd like to tell you a little about my aunt so you'll be prepared," he said.

I shifted in my seat so that I faced him. "You make her sound like an ogre."

"I don't mean to. As you know, she was great in her day and she is completely unsympathetic to modern ballet. She insists on going, though . . . sometimes I think she secretly admires the change, but is too stubborn to admit it. Her opinion is that you're tops. Her favorite male dancer is Oriano."

"She must be delighted that he is dancing here."

"She is. She's also quite impressed with Mirabel Rousseau."

"But Mirabel writes only contemporary ballets," I exclaimed.

"Exactly." He turned on the motor, backed the car onto the road, and we continued on our way. "That's my aunt. You may find her puzzling and exasperating, but you'll not find her dull. That I guarantee."

"I'm fascinated," I said. "And impatient to meet her."

"We're entering what's known locally as Incline Village. Auntie lives well above it. She likes isolation, as you'll see."

We climbed steadily over the narrow road until we finally reached the top of a ridge. From there, Steve turned into a forked road that was rutted and bumpy and apparently little used.

I was startled by my first glimpse of the house, which might have been set in the midst of a Bavarian forest, a castle occupied by at least a baron. It was three stories high, a huge, sprawling place of many gables and turrets. The windows were narrow, deep-set and tall. It was centered in the midst of enormously tall pines which shaded it, probably making its interior gloomy.

"Spooky-looking, isn't it?" he asked.

"Yes," I agreed. "But intriguing. I'm impatient to see it."

Looking pleased, he pulled up before the marble-pillared, tiled portico. A Rolls Royce was already parked there.

"Auntie's car," he told me. "A 1951. In a few more years she'll probably have ten thousand miles on it."

He helped me out and we walked around the Rolls.

"Does she drive?" I asked.

"Oh, yes. Though not often. She's had the car out today, though, and apparently intends to go out again. She has no servants living in. A married couple who live in the village come twice a week. Since she's alone here, it's sufficient help."

THREE

As we neared the oversized double doors, one of them swung open and a woman dressed in black chiffon emerged. Both her arms were outstretched toward Steve. She embraced him and he kissed her cheek. I knew she must be about seventy-five, yet her face was unlined and there was a sparkle to her unfaded blue eyes. Her hair was white and worn piled high on her head, but her figure had the sleekness of a girl in her twenties.

She turned from Steve to me and the smile of welcome she had for her nephew now encompassed me. She embraced me and kissed me on the cheek, then held me at arm's length to observe me more closely.

"Nicolette Artaude. Not quite as tall as I thought, but beautifully proportioned. I've seen you perform many times and have always found your performances stimulating."

"Thank you, Miss Davina."

"Call me Amorita, my dear. I hear my name spoken little enough these days. What may I call you?"

"Nicki," Steve broke in. "And I have to talk with you, Auntie."

She waved a hand disdainfully. "Run along and make some house calls. I want to get acquainted with Nicki."

"I'll go shortly, but something happened during rehearsal at the cabaret you should know about."

The remark sobered her. "What do you mean?"

Steve told her about the sandbag and the broken boards. She looked neither surprised nor angry at the revelation.

"I had that entire place checked," she said. "I realized it was old and had been long unused. I also had the floor carefully examined."

"I know you did," Steve said. "I don't know if the stage was tampered with, but I do know that the rope on the sandbag was cut."

"Come into the drawing room," she said, "and pour us each a glass of sherry. Who would do such a vile thing?"

She led the way through the large gloomy reception hall into a circular room, so large that parts of it seemed lost in the shadowy reaches. The dark, massive furniture added to the cheerlessness of the place. Castle Morvant seemed an oddly melancholy home for a woman of such vivacity, I reflected.

Steve poured sherry into two glasses and brought them to us. I felt no need for another, but I took it, sensing that his aunt would be hurt if I refused.

She addressed her nephew. "Now that you've told me the bad news you brought, you may make your house calls."

His smile was tolerant and he gave me an apologetic glance. "I'll be back in a couple of hours."

"Run along," Amorita commanded. "We have no need of you. We wish to discuss ballet and you know nothing about it. Go."

26

"Guess I'd better," he said with a grin. He waved a farewell and left the room. I heard the low purr of the motor as he guided his car along the drive to the winding road. Amorita's head was tilted in an attentive attitude and a smile touched her lips as our eyes met.

"Despite my bullying, I do love him, you know," she said. "He's a very dedicated doctor and a brilliant one. Crystal City is lucky to have him. He should be in a big city, where his skill would be appreciated. He claims the lake has charmed him and he'll not leave it. I'm sure it's because he feels he'd be deserting this old lady . . . who is tough and quite capable of taking care of herself."

"He knows that," I said. "Did it ever occur to you it could be love for you that keeps him here?"

She regarded me with new interest. "You're not afraid of me, are you?"

"Not in the least."

"Humph. Guess I *am* getting old. Oh, I know Steve loves me. I just don't want anyone to think I'm in my dotage. Did you know Steve is licensed in California and Nevada? One has to be here—the state lines run through the middle of everything. Now tell me about the ballet you're acting in. I hate the modern ones. I know today it's called the generation gap when you don't go along, but to me, ballet means being on one's toes."

"But there is just so much one can do on one's toes."

"I suppose," she said reluctantly. "But I still don't like it."

"Then why do you still attend?"

"So Steve told you he ferries me around," she retorted grudgingly. "I should say 'flies'. I hate the damn planes. Scare me half to death."

"I love flying," I said. "And I'll bet you do too, though you'll not admit it."

"Fiddlesticks." She pointed a forefinger at me. "When you say that there is only so much one can do on one's toes, are you trying to tell me I couldn't dance as well as you or any prima ballerina today?"

"Indeed not." I set down my glass on the table alongside me. "From what I've read of you, I could never equal your pirouettes or your entrechats. And your bal penchés—the way you leaped horizontally and then turned in mid-air. I know nothing has been seen like it since."

"Nor ever will be," she averred. "I respect Theo Coubet, but he's too old to be going for that modern stuff."

"You know, the very fact that he goes for it has kept him young," I argued. I could see that Amorita would overwhelm me if I let her.

"It's apparent I'll get no place with you." She regarded me in silence for a few moments. "Tell you what. Where are you staying?"

"The entire cast is at the Spindle Motel."

"You're going to check out and live here. I can think of no other way to convince you that the ballet as it was, is far better than the crazy things they do today."

I laughed. "If that's your reason for inviting me to live with you, forget it. You'd be wasting your time—and mine."

She joined me in laughter. "I'm joking, my dear. I am a harridan, but I am also a lonely old woman. Please come live with me. Perhaps there is something I can teach you. The bal penchés, for instance. It was skill, yes—but there's a trick to it as well. Please."

"You make it very difficult for me to refuse," I said. "Perhaps more difficult if I say you might even convert me to believing the modern ballet is more interesting, diversified, and exciting than something like *Swan Lake*."

"I think you're a fraud. I don't believe you need one iota of convincing. You know it, but you just won't admit it."

"That's something we can argue about," she said complacently, knowing I'd agree to come here. "Now tell me about the ballet you're going to do. First of all, the name."

I did that, going into detail about the plot. She listened politely until I'd finished. A few times I detected a flicker of annoyance cross her face, but just as quickly her features assumed again a look of polite interest.

"The Lorraine Brewster case," she said, searching her mind for facts. "I recall something about it. Happened in California, didn't it? About two years ago. One of those fantastic things that newspaper people dote on, and keep writing about, weeks after it's all over. Yes . . . as I recall, there was a mention of ghosts."

"Do you believe in them?" I asked.

"Of course I do. Don't you?"

"No."

"There are times when I think this castle is haunted. Perhaps I shouldn't say that. It might scare you away."

"It won't. I don't believe in the supernatural. Tell me, why have you isolated yourself so completely from your profession? You could still contribute a great deal."

"You're very kind, but I think you're in error. The young people would ridicule me." She gave a delicate shrug of her shoulders. "They'd regard me as another old lady trying to foist her ideas on them. No—I'll continue to live here with my memories. They're more precious than jewels." Her voice had become quite emotional and she paused for a few moments to regain control. "How is Theo?"

"He's well, and still a brilliant choreographer."

"We danced together, you know."

"I *wish* I could have seen you," I said sincerely. "It must have been marvelous."

She looked pleased and we went into a lengthy discussion of the ballet theater and its people. And it wasn't all talk of the past; she knew a great deal of what was going on today. I suspected she subscribed to trade journals and read them avidly.

We were still at it, comparing the classic with the modern techniques, when Steve returned. He seemed delighted with the idea of my staying at his aunt's.

"It will be good for both of you, but even better for me," he said.

His aunt's brows raised inquisitively. "Just how do you figure that?"

"It will give me a better opportunity to see Nicki."

"Between rehearsals and your possessive aunt, I doubt she'll have much time for you." Amorita softened her words with a smile.

He laughed. "You're bossy, but not possessive. Since you had to raise me, I know."

I stood up. "I'm looking forward to being your guest, Amorita."

"Hurry back," she said. "I'll walk you to the car."

"I'm taking her to dinner," Steve replied. "I'm also going to loan her my Volks. That is, if you drive, Nicki."

"I do," I said. "I have a car in New York—though I mostly use it to get to the country. My parents left me a house in a small town at the foot of the Berkshires."

"Where are you staying?"

"The Spindle Motel."

"I could chauffeur Nicki," Amorita said. "In fact, I'd like to. It would give me an excuse to observe her rehearsals."

"You don't need an excuse," I told her. "We'd be honored with your presence."

"And Nicki doesn't need a chauffeur," Steve replied sensibly. "She's using my car."

"Just as well," Amorita agreed complacently. "I don't care too much about rising early any more."

Steve addressed his aunt, who had accompanied us outside. "Want me to garage your car?"

"Indeed not. I'll probably go out again."

"Twice in one day?" Steve asked in obvious surprise.

30

She gave him an impatient glance. "Do I have to make an accounting to you every time I go out?"

"Don't start getting uppity. I'm delighted to see you get out of this gloomy dungeon."

"It's my sanctuary," she replied disdainfully. "But it so happens I've been invited out for an early dinner."

Steve said, "Good for you."

She waved to us as we drove off. Though Steve drove cautiously along the narrow, winding road, he lost no time in reaching the motel. I told him we'd start rehearsing at nine tomorrow morning, providing the floor was repaired.

"I hope my aunt remembers to attend to it," he said.

"Don't worry," I replied serenely. "Theodoric will attend to it. Mirabel won't give him a moment's peace until he does."

FOUR

Steve remained in the car while I went to my room. On the way, I met Mirabel. She looked relieved to see me.

"Where were you, Nicki?"

"I was visiting Amorita Davina," I replied.

She looked puzzled. "So were we."

"At Castle Morvant? This afternoon?"

"Yes. She was at the motel when we got back and she invited Theo, Oriano, Holly and me up for cocktails. Theo rode with her. Holly and I went with Oriano."

"She didn't mention your having been there," I said.

"Well, we were and she took us on a Cook's tour of the place." Mirabel shuddered. "I wouldn't care to live there."

I smiled. "She invited me to be her guest while we're up here."

"Did you accept?"

I nodded. "I'm really excited about it."

"You should be." Mirabel looked almost envious. "She's quite a gal."

"Her nephew, Steve Fenmore, is waiting for me outside."

"Is he bringing you back there?"

"No," I replied. "But he's loaning me a Volks. I'll need it to make the trips back and forth."

"You certainly will," Mirabel said. "We told Amorita about the loose floorboards on the stage and she gave Theodoric the name of the man to contact in town. He's already at work on them."

I suddenly remembered the sandbag. "Something else happened."

"At the cabaret?"

I nodded and went into detail about it. Her face colored with anger when I told her Steve's inspection of the rope revealed it had been cut.

"Who could have done such a thing?" she exclaimed.

"I can't imagine," I said. I again thought of Holly, but I still couldn't believe she'd resort to murder to gain the role of prima ballerina. "Steve—Dr. Fenmore—said that maybe someone was using the cabaret as a shelter, and cut the rope in an effort to frighten us away."

Her brow furrowed. "I wonder if those floorboards were deliberately tampered with. Amorita said she'd had the entire place inspected before our arrival."

"Steve told me the same thing."

"How did you get acquainted with her nephew?"

I smiled. "When the sandbag fell, I panicked and ran from the theater, practically colliding with him in the lobby. He came with an invitation from his aunt, requesting that I pay her a visit."

Mirabel looked perplexed. "Strange she didn't mention that to us."

I shrugged. "She may be a little eccentric. She didn't

tell me you'd been there, or admit that she already knew about the broken boards on the stage."

Mirabel said, "She's having dinner with Theo."

"Where Oriano is dancing?"

"No. She mentioned a place that's quiet and rustic. I believe she wants to reminisce."

It sounded logical. "Did you know she prefers classic ballet to modern?"

Mirabel's smile indicated she well knew. "When I told her about the *Ballad of Lorraine*, she dismissed it with an impatient wave of her hand."

"Perhaps we'll convert her," I said hopefully.

Mirabel's laughter was hearty and infectious. "I think it's worth a try. I invited her to rehearsals."

"So did I," I said. "I felt you wouldn't object."

"I'd like it very much," Mirabel confessed. "I think it would spur the cast to outdo themselves."

"It's worth a try," I said. "I must run along now. Rehearsal at nine tomorrow?"

"If the floor is repaired," Mirabel said.

"I'm sure Amorita will see to it. Are you going to the casino to watch Oriano?"

"For a while. See you tomorrow."

I went to my room and hastily packed my belongings. It didn't take long, for I'd had a lot of practice. Also, I hadn't brought a great many things along, knowing I'd spend most of my time in my rehearsal clothes.

Steve was out of the car when he caught sight of me coming through the small lobby. He deposited the bags in the trunk of the car and drove directly to an inn in the midst of pines. The air was brisk now, for it was almost dark, but stimulating and fresh.

The inn was only partially filled because it was still early. We had a table looking out on the lake. We ordered immediately, not bothering with cocktails, for Steve had to make two house calls, so there wasn't time for lingering. I didn't mind, though I found myself enjoying his company. The way he regarded me as I spoke made me feel as if my most inconsequential statement was intensely interesting. Also, he had an easy smile which I found myself returning.

"Is there anyone special in your life?" he asked. "I mean romantically."

"No one," I replied.

"I'll remember that—hopefully."

"You mean you have no attachments?" I asked, genuinely surprised.

"None," he replied. "I love medicine and I've devoted most of my time to it."

"Do you specialize?"

"In every branch of medicine. My card states I'm a family physician. Also, I make house calls."

"That's unusual," I said. "You should be in great demand."

"Let's talk about you," he said. "Did you grow up in Connecticut?"

"Yes. My parents died a year ago. An automobile accident."

"I'm sorry. I lost mine when I was still a toddler. Amorita stepped in and filled the breach. It was dear of her because she was no longer young, but my mother was her favorite niece."

I said, "I was surprised to learn Mirabel and Theodoric, along with Holly Larkin and Oriano, were guests at Castle Morvant this afternoon."

"My aunt must have invited them."

"She did," I said. "She was waiting at the motel when they returned. What puzzles me is why she sent you to invite me. Had I returned to the motel, I'm sure I'd have been invited along with the others."

"And if we'd gone directly to my aunt's from the cabaret, we'd have met the others there."

"What are you saying?"

35

"Just this. My aunt's eccentric, sometimes. Don't be surprised at anything she does."

I nodded. "I guess I'd better not be, though it seems odd that when you told her about the floor, she didn't give the slightest hint she knew about it."

"As I said, she's eccentric. Would you rather not be with her?"

His manner was more concern for me than resentment at my bewilderment regarding his aunt.

"Oh no," I said. "I like her. She's interesting. Incidentally, she took no pains to conceal the fact that she completely detests contemporary ballet."

"I think she enjoys castigating it," he said. "Confidentially, she never misses one. She flies to San Francisco and Los Angeles just to see them, though that's in confidence also."

"I'm glad to hear it," I said. "Now I must be getting along. You have calls to make and I want to get my rest. Tomorrow will be an arduous day, I know."

"Can you find your way back?" he asked.

"Oh yes," I said. "I already studied the landmarks leading to Castle Morvant."

"Good." He motioned the waitress for the check. "I'll drive you to my place and put your luggage in the Volks."

"Thanks, Steve. You've been very kind."

"Just a preview of things to come," he said in mock seriousness.

His apartment was new, modern, and of the garden type. He drove around to the rear, transferred my luggage to the Volkswagen, and gave me the keys. I backed the car from its stall, turned it around, and waved a farewell. I was delighted at the prospect of having a car and I had no trouble getting back to the road which led to Incline Village, but I was glad when the car completed the climb and I stopped before the portico of

Castle Morvant, for the night was starless and there was a definite chill in the air.

Dim light shone through the windows on the first floor, but what surprised me was that the double entrance doors were opened wide. Beyond, I could see a cheery fire burning in the massive fireplace. It helped to dispel the dreary aspect of the place, yet if that was Amorita's idea of welcoming me, it was eccentric, to say the least. And a waste of firewood.

I left the car in the front, for I didn't knew exactly where the garage was situated. I decided the wisest course would be to check with Amorita.

I brought my bags inside, set them down, and called out her name. There was no answer and my voice seemed to ring hollowly, as if I were in a vast cavern. I called to her again and when there was still no response, I began to worry. She was in her seventies. Something could have happened to her. Certainly she wouldn't have gone off, leaving the front doors wide open.

The cavernous rooms were lighted, but dimly. I went into the drawing room and walked to the far end of it, checking to see whether she'd fallen and was hidden by a piece of furniture. I searched the dining room and the library and entered the huge kitchen. I opened the door leading to the grounds at the rear, calling her name again and again, but to no avail. Getting steadily more concerned, I ran upstairs. There were seven bedrooms, all large. I checked each, but found no trace of her. I discovered a narrow, steep staircase leading to the third floor, climbed it, and stepped into an enormous attic, strewn with odd pieces of furniture and trunks which probably held Amorita's costumes.

The only light was from an old, discarded chandelier, suspended from the ceiling in the center of the room. It spread the light rather thinly, or perhaps the bulb in it was small. But the fact that it was lit assured me that Amorita had come up here.

Quickly scanning the room, I noticed a door at the far end, partially open. I went to it and saw that it led into what seemed to be a vault. In it hung furs of several types. Relics of Amorita's past. And there, on the floor, covered with a mound of furs, I thought I'd found her. Praying that she wasn't dead, I ran into the small room, knelt and threw aside the furs. There was nothing beneath them. I had been panicked by a pile of old furs that vaguely resembled a body.

Then I thought the light went out, but it was more than that. The door had closed with a heavy thud and I was in total darkness. I moved cautiously, arms outstretched, trying to reach the door. I fumbled for the knob and turned it, but the door didn't move. I tried once again before I realized the door had not only slammed shut, but was locked. There was no way I could get out.

FIVE

I told myself to be calm, that someone would come at any moment to rescue me. Certainly, the entire castle wouldn't be lighted, however dimly, if no one was about. I reminded myself of the front doors opened wide, as if in a welcoming gesture. Amorita, I recalled, had said she had an early dinner engagement. If my reasoning was correct, she'd return soon and once she saw my car parked, my baggage in the hall, she'd begin looking for me. I pounded on the door, paused, and pounded again. I had no idea how much time had passed, but I realized I was beginning to breathe deeply as my lungs clamored for air in this small, fur-filled closet.

I supposed it was airtight as a protection against moths. I began to feel a little light-headed. Was I going to suffocate in this small room, sealed off from the rest of the world?

My cheek was pressed against the door and I still

pounded on it with the palms of my hands. I even kicked at it with my feet. I called out for help, over and over, but I had to stop because it involved using too much oxygen and I sensed there was precious little left.

I took a few backward steps and my legs came in contact with the pile of furs. I eased myself down on them, thinking in despair that at least I'd have a soft bed to die on. I prayed that Amorita would return before I used all the oxygen in the room.

I knew I had to remain perfectly still, keep my breathing shallow if I could and, above all, not panic. That would be the most foolish thing I could do, for I'd burn up what little oxygen was left, in a matter of minutes. But if I kept still, how would anyone know I was trapped here?

Then another thought sent a fresh shiver of fear through me. Had the door closed by itself—or had someone pushed it shut? Someone could have been hiding in the attic-like third floor, concealed behind a piece of furniture or a trunk, awaiting me and feeling a sense of triumph that I'd been lured up here in my search for Amorita, only to be caught in a trap that could end in my death.

I tried to dismiss the thought as foolish, but I could not. What had happened on the stage with the sandbag was not an accident. So why should the closing of this door have been accidental?

But why would anybody want to kill me? I had no enemies, I owned nothing anybody would covet. Jealousy could be a motive, perhaps, and in the field of the ballet jealousies do exist, but no one ever committed murder because of it.

I even fell to wondering if Amorita Davina was responsible. She'd gone to great lengths to tell me how much she resented the new ballet. Yet that seemed implausible. Steve was in almost daily contact with her and would have noticed any mental abberation.

The air was growing fetid. I wondered how much longer I had left before the coughing and the choking began. I got up, moved cautiously to the door and pounded halfheartedly on it again, kicked it a few times, and wondered how long I'd been locked in here.

I was just going to go back to my bed of furs when the door opened and Amorita, her features expressing amazement, stared at me.

"What *are* you doing up here?" Irritation edged her voice.

I ignored her question and reeled dizzily past her into the attic, my lungs gasping for air. I leaned weakly against a large table and started to cry. Apparently she realized what had happened and went over to a window and raised it, then returned and led me over to it, easing me onto a straight-back chair.

"Here, take this," she ordered, handing me a handkerchief. I thanked her and sat motionless until I felt myself again.

"What happened, Nicki?" Her voice had softened.

"I'm not sure exactly," I looked up at her.

Her concern seemed genuine; her smile, apologetic. "I'm sorry I was rude. But why in the world did you come up here?"

"I was looking for you," I told her quietly.

"Because I left the front doors unlocked?" she asked. "I told you I had an early dinner engagement. I didn't know if Steve would accompany you back. If he didn't, you'd not get in otherwise."

"Did you leave the doors open wide?" I asked.

"Of course not. That would be foolish."

"Did you leave a light on in every room in the house?"

"There'd be small need for that. I assumed you'd wait downstairs, if you returned before me."

"I certainly would have." My voice carried more res-

41

onance now that my strength had returned. "But both entrance doors were opened wide. I thought it odd, particularly in view of the blazing fireplace which couldn't warm the hall with all the cold air coming in. I closed the doors and went through the first floor searching for you and calling your name. Then I went upstairs and inspected each bedroom. There was a light in every room."

I felt she believed me, though she appeared bewildered by what I said. "Go on, my dear."

"So I came up here. I found the door to your fur vault open and a pile of furs on the floor. I thought you'd fallen and the furs concealed you. When I started to toss aside the furs, the door closed. I tried to open it, but it was locked. I banged on it with my hands, kicked it, and cried for help. I think I was in there quite a while. At least it seemed so. Breathing became quite an effort."

"Do you feel well enough to come downstairs? I'll call Steve."

"Oh, please don't bother him," I said. "I'll be all right now."

"We'll let him determine that." She spoke with quiet firmness.

I stood up and she placed an arm around my waist, guiding me to the stairway. At the foot, she snapped the switch, plunging the attic into darkness. Neither of us spoke until we reached the drawing room. There, she insisted I lie down. She made a call to Steve, then returned and poured a glass of sherry for me, urging me to sip it. I'd have rather just sat quietly, but I knew she was making amends for her curt manner when she discovered me.

"Steve is coming immediately." She sat down opposite me. "Now I'll talk. I was quite surprised when I returned to find the entire castle illuminated. Not that I'm complaining about your use of electricity, but I was piqued that you'd go on an inspection tour of the place when I was out."

"I did go on an inspection tour," I replied, "but only because I was worried about you. However, as I told you. I closed the doors downstairs, but I didn't put the lights out in any of the rooms since I didn't know if you wished them on. All during my search, I kept calling your name. When I didn't find you, I sought the stairway to the attic. The lights were on there, too. I'm afraid I was lured up there by someone for the sole purpose of locking me in that closet."

A fleeting smile touched her lips. "My dear, the door was not locked."

"It was," I exclaimed impatiently. "I tried my best to open it."

"Well . . ." her hands raised expressively and dropped into her lap. "When I returned and saw the castle lit up, I made an inspection, particularly when I saw the lights in the attic. On my way up the stairs, I heard you kicking the door. Thank goodness I did. But you needed only to turn the knob and the door would have opened for you."

I started to contradict her, but decided against it. I was too grateful to argue further; if the attic light hadn't been on, I'd still be lying in that small room, unconscious by now.

By the time Steve arrived, I was myself again. He insisted on examining me, but found nothing wrong. He sat down beside his aunt and addressed me.

"Now tell me exactly what happened."

I repeated almost verbatim what I'd told his aunt.

He turned to her. "Did you place the furs on the floor?"

"Certainly not," she exclaimed indignantly. "And I hope they're not still there."

"I'll go up and see," Steve said.

"They're still there," I said, though Steve was already out of the room. "I didn't hang them up."

"It doesn't make sense," Amorita said. "It just doesn't make sense."

"It doesn't to me either," I said. "I don't know why someone would want to kill me, but it's obvious someone does."

"But why, my dear?" Amorita exclaimed.

"I haven't the faintest idea," I said. "Certainly the sandbag was no accident."

"Probably not," she agreed. "But it may not have been meant for you. It could have fallen on any other member of the cast. You just happened to be sitting there at the time."

"And I just happened to come up here tonight," I said.

"Drink your sherry, my dear," she urged. "It will calm you."

I'd set the untouched glass down, but I picked it up and obediently took a sip.

Amorita eyed me quizzically. "I hope you don't think I lured you up to the attic with murderous intent—since you apparently believe someone did."

"What else can I believe?" I asked.

"You *do* think I am trying to kill you?" she demanded indignantly.

"Of course I don't," I exclaimed. "I know you couldn't have been here."

Steve came in then, looking vaguely uncomfortable.

"What is it?" I asked.

"The door of the vault was still ajar, but there were no furs on the floor." He patted his coat pocket. "I carry a small pocket flash and I checked carefully."

"But there were," I contradicted. "You must have seen them, Amorita."

Her smile was apologetic. "I'm sorry, my dear. When you staggered out of there, I thought only of your well-being."

"And you didn't see the pile of furs on the floor?" My voice was almost a plea.

She moved her head from side to side. "And the door was not locked. All you had to do was turn the knob and walk out."

"It *was* locked," I protested. "I tried the knob when the door first closed on me. It wouldn't budge. I kicked at it and hit it and cried out for help until I felt myself growing faint from lack of air. That was when I went over and sat on the pile of furs." I turned to Steve. "I thought your aunt lay beneath them. They were placed in such a way as to make it seem that they concealed a body. I had just started to toss them aside when the door slammed, though by then I knew there was nobody underneath the furs."

Amorita said, "I know you were trying to attract attention by banging the door because I heard you. But I repeat, Nicki, the door was not locked."

"Then someone was up there and unlocked it," I said. "I'll admit I didn't try the knob after the first few minutes, but I swear the door was locked. Also," I added, for Steve's benefit, "when I reached the castle, both entrance doors were opened wide. Don't you think that strange, since your aunt wasn't even here?"

Steve addressed his aunt. "Where were you?"

"I told you I had an early dinner engagement." She spoke with a trace of annoyance. "I suppose you wish to know the name of my escort."

"Any reason why you shouldn't tell us?" Steve asked, a smile tinging his lips.

"Theodoric Coubet." Amorita spoke with an injured air. "He was with me every minute and he did not come up here."

"You needn't sulk, Auntie," Steve said. "No one's accusing you or Theodoric Coubet of trying to frighten Nicki."

"I should hope not," she said indignantly. "The moment I returned I began searching the castle because I could see, even before I reached it, lights in all the windows, even the attic. And a good thing I noticed them up there. I'd never have thought of checking the attic otherwise."

"Not even when the Volks was outside?" Steve asked.

"I'm afraid not. If Nicki wasn't about, I'd have thought you came back with her and took her to dinner."

"I did take her to dinner," Steve said. "Anyway, she's safe now. I'm concerned, though, about what's been happening to her."

Amorita moved a large pearl ring on and off her index finger. Without meeting my eyes, she said, "Nicki, you say the door was locked. I found it open. You say there was a pile of furs on the floor and you feared I might be underneath them. Yet Steve found no evidence of their being disturbed."

"Someone hung them up after you and I left the attic."

"And the locked door?" Amorita asked.

"Whoever locked it, unlocked it," I replied.

"It doesn't make sense," she said.

I contained my annoyance. "Perhaps not, but I'm telling the truth. Do you believe me, Steve?"

"Yes," he said.

"You hesitated," I said. "Why?"

"I'm sorry," he said. "I do believe you. I saw the rope which supported the sandbag. It had been deliberately cut. You didn't lie about that. There were loose floorboards on the stage. Perhaps they were there all the time. I don't know."

"I'd forgotten about them," Amorita mused. "They were not there. I know. I checked that floor and you were with me, Steve."

He nodded agreement.

"My dear,"—her manner became solicitous again—"forgive me. I will believe everything you said."

Steve said, "Perhaps whoever locked you in the closet

46

heard Auntie returning and panicked, but before leaving, unlocked the door."

"But who hung up the furs?" I asked.

"Did you go back up there, Amorita?" Steve asked.

Her eyes flashed indignantly. "I did not."

"Then I'd better make a search of the place," Steve said. "And I'm taking Nicki back to town with me. I doubt she's safe here."

Amorita looked so crushed I felt she'd taken it as a personal affront. I knew she was on the verge of tears.

I got up and went over to her, covering her hands with one of mine. "Don't be hurt, please."

She blinked hard to hold back the tears. "I did so want you to stay. And I still do."

"Then I'll stay," I said.

"Steve won't let you."

"Yes, he will. Unless he won't let you stay either."

"This is my home. I'm not afraid. And I'll not be taken from it."

Steve was already upstairs and we could hear him opening and closing doors as he moved from room to room. After about fifteen minutes he returned to the first floor, checked that, and rejoined us.

He said, "I searched the attic and the bedrooms and there isn't a trace of anyone having been here. And certainly we're the only ones in this castle now."

"Then may Nicki stay?" Amorita entreated.

"No," Steve said firmly.

"Please," I pleaded. "I want to. I'm over my fright and whoever did that apparently had second thoughts when he unlocked the door of the fur vault."

"And also hung up the furs to cast doubt on your story," he reasoned. "I think the police should be notified."

"Please don't," I said. "Perhaps this will end it."

"Perhaps it won't," he contradicted. "The next time you may not be so lucky."

"Listen to her, Steve," Amorita added her pleas to mine. "Unfavorable publicity will do the show no good. It could even place a jinx on it."

"I should think you'd be in favor of that," he retorted, "since you dislike contemporary ballet."

"But I love the performers," she replied. "And I don't like to see them hurt."

"I don't want to see Nicki hurt," he countered.

"I won't be, Steve," I said. "I'll be on guard now."

He stood in reflective silence for a moment. Both Amorita and I regarded him hopefully, willing him to relent.

Amorita said, "I have a gun, Steve, and I know how to use it."

He still looked dubious. "Is there any feuding going on among the cast members? Specifically with you?"

"Not really," I told him. "I told you that Holly Larkin wants to be prima ballerina, and makes no secret of the fact that she'll stop at nothing to get it. Nothing, that is, short of murder."

"Did she threaten you?"

"No," I exclaimed.

Amorita said flatly, "She only wished you'd break an arm or a leg."

"How did you know?" I asked in surprise.

She gave me a knowing glance. "My dear, I was there once."

I laughed and she joined me, but Steve remained serious. "If you won't let me go to the police, then come back to the Spindle Motel. I feel you'll be safer there."

"I want to stay with your aunt," I said. "I like it here. I may never have another opportunity to live in a castle."

"All right." He conceded defeat. "Just so long as you *live* in it. But do be watchful and keep the doors locked, Auntie."

"Don't worry about that," Amorita said firmly. "And thanks for letting Nicki stay."

"It's against my better judgment," he said. "But since it's what you both want, I'll go along with it. Just keep the doors locked."

"Don't worry about that," Amorita said. "I'll follow you to the door and slip the heavy burglar chain in place after you leave—which will be now."

He glanced at me and sighed. "I guess that's that."

I smiled, pleased at his reluctance to go. "Your aunt knows ballerinas need lots of rest."

"Exactly," Amorita said, leading the way to the door. "Come along, Steve."

I got up. "I'll walk to the door with you."

His hands gripped my shoulders lightly. "No, you'll stay right here. I might be tempted to take you with me."

Without further ado, he bent and kissed me lightly on the lips. "Take care, Nicki. And I believe everything you said happened.

"Thanks, Steve." My heart warmed with gratitude, but I didn't say more, for words seemed to fail me. I hadn't expected his brief kiss to have such an effect on me.

SIX

Amorita returned to the room just as the sound of Steve's motor roared into life. Glancing at my untouched glass of sherry, she urged me to drink it.

"I'm sorry, Amorita," I said. "I felt it wouldn't agree with me."

"Then you must have a cup of hot chocolate," she said. "Tell you what. I'll bring you to your room. You can undress, slip into a robe, and we'll have it before the fireplace in the hall. There are two green velvet chairs there, very warm, very soft, and we can snuggle into them while we sip our chocolate."

"Please don't bother," I said. I wanted nothing more than to get into bed and relax my tense muscles. I was beginning to feel the chill of the castle and knew I must get into leg warmers. I couldn't risk having my muscles tighten up.

"It will be no bother," she said crisply. "Come along,

my dear. I'll keep you up only long enough to drink your chocolate."

I was beginning to realize that she was accustomed to having her own way and if I was going to achieve any degree of independence, I was going to have to stand up to her. However, tonight I decided to give in. The thought of the warm beverage did sound good.

I picked up my luggage and followed her up the stairs. She led me to one of the bedrooms I'd inspected, but hadn't noticed in regard to its furnishings. I was pleasantly surprised to observe the furniture was dainty and colorful. The wood was an oyster gray with flowers painted over its surface. The bed was canopied and curtained in pink silk, with matching window draperies. I complimented her on its cheerfulness.

"I had it made up specially for me when I was young," she said. "It's a room for a young girl. That's why I no longer use it."

A photograph in a silver frame of a young man in a World War I uniform sat on a table by the bed.

Amorita said, "He was my fiancé. My first and only love—killed in France."

"I'm sorry, Amorita."

"The agony left me long ago, but I still have my memories. As one gets older, they become more precious. Now change into night clothes and come downstairs."

She left me then and I quickly unpacked my bags and donned a soft fleece, ankle-length nightie and warm woolen robe. I pulled on woolen leg warmers which reached from my ankles to my thighs. They were bulky and ugly, but quite necessary for a ballerina. I slipped my feet into ankle-high, brushed-nylon, soft-soled shoes which I called bunnies, and returned downstairs.

Amorita had a small table set up before the glowing fireplace. On it was a silver service and a dish of small cookies. She motioned me to one of the velvet chairs and she took the other. We were both warm and comfortable. She poured chocolate into each of the cups, offered me the dish of cookies and we settled back to enjoy our snack.

"Tell me, my dear, about this Holly Larkin."

"What do you wish to know about her?" I asked.

"First, describe her."

I did briefly. When I finished, she said, "With her coloring, she's a good foil for you. I am looking forward to meeting her."

I eyed her with new awareness because it suddenly occurred to me that they had already met. My tone was sharp as I said, "You're playing a game with me, Amorita. Why?"

Her brows raised questioningly. "I don't understand."

"Then I'll tell you. Holly was here this afternoon along with Oriano, Mirabel, and Theodoric."

Her eyes held a hint of mischief. "So you know."

"Mirabel told me," I said. "Why didn't you tell Steve you already knew about the boards on the stage when we came this afternoon?"

She gave a subtle shrug of her shoulders. "I fear I have a fondness for melodrama."

"Is that what you call it?" I asked coldly.

"What would you call it?" She seemed completely nonplussed by my accusation.

"Deceit, guile, even trickery."

"Oh, come now, Nicki. Aren't you being a little too sanctimonious?"

"No." I set my cup and saucer on the table. "If I'd known you enjoyed playing these kinds of games, I'd not have stayed."

"Please, my dear," she said. "Forgive the vagaries of an old woman. I did deceive you. If you had returned to the motel with the others, I'd have included you in the invitation."

"You had already sent your nephew with an invitation for me to visit you," I reminded her.

She nodded. "I have read where you keep to yourself quite a bit. I feared you might refuse were I to ask it, but I knew he would plead my cause. He's a doctor and he has a gentle way about him; also, he loves me. Because of the latter, he overlooks many of my weaknesses."

I regarded her coldly. "Did you shut me in the vault upstairs?"

"I swear I did not. I don't play practical jokes. I really want you here. I'm a great admirer of yours. Also, I'm lonely. My decision to go to the Spindle was quite spontaneous. I've known Theodoric for a long time. I read quite a bit about Mirabel Rousseau. And, of course, Oriano. As for Holly, she was a stranger—that is, in the sense of having a name in the ballet."

"She won't be for long," I replied. "She's a brilliant dancer and she'll go to the top."

"I'm sure of it," she said. "The little I talked with her made me aware of her supreme ego and drive. While it might be trying as a daily diet, it's a great help when one seeks a career in the entertainment world. Do you think she might have come up here and shut you in the vault?"

"She probably didn't even know about it," I said.

"Oh yes, she did. I brought the four of them up to see the view. It's quite spectacular. Oriano was curious about the door and what was behind it. I opened it and showed them some of my furs. Most of them are quite old-fashioned, and we got some laughs out of them." She paused, then added hopefully, "Do you forgive me?"

Without hesitation, I said, "Yes." I sensed her loneliness and knew she'd meant nothing vicious, though I still had some reservations regarding her. It could well have been she who had locked me in the fur vault. I wondered if there might be a touch of senility which Steve wasn't aware of. To her, it might be a child's game.

We sat there for over an hour and I listened, entranced by her stories of her past and her knowledge of present-day ballet. There was no infirmity of the mind where that was concerned. At last we got up and carried the dishes to the kitchen, which was a blend of chrome and porcelain. It was modern in every respect, in contrast to the other rooms downstairs.

I noticed the chain fastened on the front door just before I turned to go upstairs. At the top, Amorita snapped off the switch, plunging the lower hall into darkness. She waited until I reached my door and opened it to allow light to flow into the hall, before she flicked off the hall switch and bade me good night. Her room was directly opposite. I held my door open until she snapped on the light switch in her room.

I was tempted to turn the key in the lock, but shrugged off my fears. Amorita was harmless—deceitful perhaps— but playing a little game, perhaps because of her loneliness. Now that she knew I was on to her, she'd probably desist. At least, I hoped it hadn't been she who'd cut the rope, loosened the floorboards of the stage and locked me in the closet. I breathed deeply of the crisp air drifting in through the open window. The tension which had gripped me even after Steve left was now abating, and as I drifted off to sleep, I thought of his kiss which, though brief, had managed to quicken my heartbeat.

I don't know what awakened me—the creaking of a floorboard or the sound of a step—but I was conscious of someone nearby. I opened my eyes enough to observe the area around my bed. There was no one close by. Easing myself onto one elbow, I looked around the room. My bedroom door was open. I strained my ears to listen and was certain I detected stealthy footsteps in the hall. Had someone been in the room and was now departing? I was more annoyed than fearful. Was it Amorita, playing another of her little games? If so, I'd surprise her at it.

I slipped from bed, pushed my feet into my bunnies, and moved cautiously to the door. My soft-soled shoes were an asset. I need only hope not to step on a board that would squeak and give me away. My luck held and I moved to the open door.

Directly opposite, the door to Amorita's room was open. I stepped into the hall and saw a figure coming up the stairs. I stood motionless, but in plain view. No lights glowed, but enough moonlight slipped through a window at the end of the hall to reveal my presence, just as I was able to view the person coming toward me.

It was a woman and as the distance between us lessened, I realized it was Amorita. I spoke her name. She turned with amazing quickness and her arm raised to reveal the silhouette of the gun she held. It was pointed directly at me.

"Don't shoot, Amorita," I pleaded. "It's Nicki."

"Oh, my dear." Her hand, holding the gun, dropped to her side. She seemed genuinely relieved. So was I, once the gun was no longer pointed at me.

I reached inside my room and snapped on the light switch. "Is something wrong?" I asked.

"I thought I heard someone moving about."

"So did I," I said. "And I found my door open. I know I shut it before I went to bed."

"I opened it," she said. "I was in your room. I checked to see if you were in bed or moving about."

"Why would I be moving about?" I asked with a trace of impatience.

"Perhaps for the same reason I was. Looking for whoever was prowling."

"I think the person I heard was you," I said. "Don't play games with me, Amorita."

"I'm not playing a game, Nicki. Please believe me."

She seemed sincere, but I knew now she was a clever actress. Yet, even in the dim light, her eyes seemed to hold more than a tinge of fear and as I spoke, she looked

55

around her as if she exepected to be confronted by some intruder.

"Suppose we inspect the house together," I said. "Room by room."

"I've already checked downstairs," she said. "The burglar chain is in place and both front and back doors are locked. The windows are closed and, I'm sure, locked. Anyway, they're so high that it wouldn't be too easy for anyone to enter through them. The ground slopes away from the house on both sides and the rear."

"Then we'll check these rooms and the attic."

"I already checked my bedroom," she said.

"And the closet?"

"There are two. I looked into both of them."

"Are there lights in them?"

"Yes. And I turned them on."

"Then we'll check the other bedrooms—*together*."

She gave me a startled look, but made no dissent. I didn't suggest it because I was afraid, but because I wanted to keep her in sight. I still couldn't be certain she wasn't up to some sort of trickery and I felt a little uneasy with the weapon she carried. The way she held it gave me the feeling she knew how to use it. However, there was no sign of an intruder nor any indication one had gained entrance.

Amorita's sigh was one of relief. "I'm glad we found no one. I'd not like to have to use this." She held up the pearl-handled revolver.

I nodded agreement. We returned to our rooms and I settled down for sleep. Yet it eluded me, for I still felt uneasy. Had Amorita really heard someone or was she playing another game? Somehow, I felt that this time she was sincere.

I was just drifting off into sleep when I thought I heard the sound of a door closing. I slipped from my bed and moved cautiously but swiftly to the window facing the road leading to the castle. I caught a brief glimpse of a figure wrapped in a cape running along the side of the road away from the house. It was impossible to tell whether it was a man or a woman, for the cape reached to the ankles and a large, wide-brimmed hat concealed the face. At this distance, I'd never have made out the features anyway.

I moved, in darkness, across the hall and quietly opened the door of Amorita's bedroom enough so that I could catch a glimpse of her form in the bed. I listened to hear her breathing. She was there. I closed the door quietly and stood in the hall, wondering who it was I'd seen and where the person had come from. I heard the sound of a motor—a putt-putt sound, like that made by a motorbike, as it roared to life. As I listened, it receded until the silence of the night once again reigned.

I went to the landing, snapped on the light switch and went down the stairs, no longer concerned about waking Amorita. I wanted to check the lock and chain on the front door.

I started to walk to the door and stopped abruptly. The chain hung free. Someone *had* opened the door. It could mean but one thing. Someone had been in here. I had heard footsteps and so had Amorita. She was not lying. Or could it be she had expected the night visitor, had gone downstairs to await him and the gun was meant to fool me? I wished Steve were closer. I'd certainly not phone him and disturb his sleep, but I hoped to see him tomorrow.

I slid the chain back in place, returned upstairs, snapped off the switch and hastened back to my bed. I lay there quietly, trying to sort things out. Slowly the answer came.

Whoever locked me in the closet hadn't had time to escape the castle. If Amorita was telling the truth, she must have returned before whoever had lured me up to the attic and imprisoned me there could get out. But where could this person have hidden? Steve searched the attic and the upstairs bedrooms. Somehow, I believed the would-be murderer had hidden himself in the attic after he unlocked the door of the closet—thus making me seem a fool when I said the door was locked.

After Amorita and I retired, the intruder came out of his hiding place, but was heard by Amorita. She got her gun and instituted a search downstairs. When she came up, she and I searched the other rooms. She said she'd already checked hers. How had we missed him? I didn't know, but I was certain of one thing now—someone didn't wish me to dance the lead role in the *Ballad of Lorraine*.

I wondered if Amorita had really been asleep when I opened the door of her room, or had been feigning it. Could it be she had an accomplice to assist her in her efforts to prevent the ballet from ever being performed? It would certainly be easy enough for Amorita to hire an accomplice. And, by so doing, she would turn suspicion away from herself.

I dared not look at the clock. I'd start worrying about how few hours of sleep I'd had. It would be better not to know.

I turned on my side and forced all thoughts of this strange day from my mind. All thoughts except those of Steve Fenmore, who had been kind and helpful and concerned. I was glad. I had no one else up here.

SEVEN

Despite the tensions of the night before, I awoke early and since Amorita was not about, I decided to drive to the motel and breakfast at the coffee shop. The Volks was still out front; I'd forgotten about garaging it. With a complete lack of traffic, I made excellent time and was delighted when I went into the restaurant and found Mirabel already seated in one of the booths. She motioned me to join her and we ordered breakfast.

Her features mirrored her concern as I told her what had happened to me at the castle. She listened in silence until I'd finished my story, then said, "What a terrible experience. Who would do such a thing?"

"I can't imagine," I said.

"It's as if someone is trying to jinx the show."

"Or doesn't want me in it," I said.

Mirabel eyed me thoughtfully. "You're referring to Holly, of course."

"No. I don't believe she'd resort to maiming me."

"Who then?" Mirabel asked.

"I wouldn't even venture a guess," I said.

"I would," she said.

"Let's talk about something more cheerful," I said.

"Let's stick to the topic you just brought up," she said firmly.

"All right," I said. "Who?"

"Amorita Davina."

"That doesn't make sense," I exclaimed, perhaps too forcefully.

"It makes a lot of sense," she replied, "and you know it."

"What do you base your accusation on?" I asked, my tone doubtful.

"On my conversation with her yesterday at the castle," she said. "Drink your orange juice, Nicki. Your poached egg will be here shortly."

I picked up the glass and sipped it dutifully. Mirabel was tackling a generous serving of melon. She'd also ordered bacon, eggs, and toast and was already on her third cup of coffee with cream.

"What did Amorita say?" I asked.

"She belittled all modern ballets and lectured us on the beauty of *Swan Lake, Les Sylphides, Sleeping Beauty,* et cetera."

I said, "I still can't see her trying to do anything that would delay our rehearsals or force cancellation of the show. She seemed delighted you rented the cabaret in which to rehearse."

"Maybe she was," Mirabel said cynically. "She couldn't be in any better position to do us harm or to cultivate us, so she'd know of our comings and goings."

"I still can't go along with your reasoning."

"Have you forgotten she invited you to live with her? *You,*"—Mirabel pointed a finger at me for emphasis—"the prima ballerina."

I shook my head. "She's lonely. She loves to talk ballet. She can even discuss contemporary ballet. I know —we sat up quite late last night and talked of nothing else."

Mirabel gave me a wry look. "Did you convince her?"

"No," I admitted. "But I believe she has an open mind about it."

"I don't," Mirabel said. "But we won't argue further about it. I'll tell Theodoric what you told me. For the present, I suggest we keep what happened to you from the rest of the cast. It might interfere with their performances. At the same time, we'll keep our eyes open."

"I know I will. But so far as Amorita Davina's contempt for modern ballet is concerned, I'm sure she's playing a game with us."

Mirabel's plump face set in tense lines. "I'm not."

I spoke with more firmness than I felt. "Steve Fenmore, her nephew, takes her to San Francisco and Los Angeles to whatever ballet is playing. Classic or contemporary, she wouldn't miss one."

"Honestly?" Mirabel's brows raised in surprise and she smiled in relief. "Well, perhaps we can eliminate her from suspicion. But who is trying to hurt you? Certainly not Theo. Nor Oriano. He's fascinated by the story. I know Holly can be nasty and has a reputation for feuding. But I've had the feeling it's a way she has of calling attention to herself. She's foolish, because she's a tremendous talent and there's no necessity for such behavior. But she enjoys being bitchy. Perhaps I'd better have a talk with her. I don't want anything to disrupt this show. I also want *you* as prima ballerina."

"I'm honored you chose me, Mirabel."

"No one else came to mind," she said matter-of-factly. "Well, here's our breakfast and I'm famished."

So was I, but I wanted a final word. "I can't believe Holly would deliberately set out to harm me. Before you

61

say anything to her, I think we should have proof of some sort."

Mirabel thought a moment, then said, "I'll go along with that, but if anything else happens, or you find evidence pointing to someone who cut that rope or locked you in that closet, promise you'll come to either Theodoric or me."

"I promise," I said quietly, hoping fervently there'd be no further incidents.

We ate in silence for a few minutes, then returned—inevitably—to the *Ballad of Lorraine*.

"I've made few changes," Mirabel confided, "because this seemed exactly right with the first draft. I even considered an ending change so you could bring the ghost of the boy you loved into human form. But I decided that would be too hard to take, and anyway, somebody has to sympathize with the ghosts. So—the boy goes back into the shadows with Holly Larkin—at least for now." She gave me a mischievous look. "Too bad, Nicki."

"I'll survive," I said glibly.

"No, you won't," she teased. "You get yours in the end—or have you forgotten?"

"No," I assured her. "I was just thinking that Holly seems to be quite smitten with Oriano."

Mirabel shrugged. "You know Oriano. I only hope she has enough sense to know he's not serious."

"I'm sure she has. Certainly she's flattered at his attention, but I believe her real reason for wanting to be with him is that during his run here, his press agent will be looking for any means of getting newspaper space for him. The fact that while working here, he's rehearsing for the ballet, will be good copy. And Holly will probably be photographed with him."

"I hope so," Mirabel mused. "It will be good publicity for us."

"And for her. By the way, is the stage fixed yet?"

Mirabel brightened. "Yes. Be ready for rehearsal at nine."

"Good. I hope we won't have any more delays."

"So do I. It's mid-October now, and I want to get out of here before the snows come. When it snows here, nothing moves. I was up here once in September visiting friends and I never saw such big snowflakes in my life, nor did I ever see it snow so hard. So we've been lucky."

We paid our checks and went outside. I invited Mirabel to ride to the cabaret with me and she eagerly consented. Short and rotund and not the least bit embarrassed by it, Mirabel, in her way, courted attention as much as Holly. Where one would expect Mirabel to choose subdued colors, she affected bright ones, plaids of brilliant hues and fabrics of wild design.

I complimented her on the red plaid pantsuit she was wearing, with a yellow turtleneck knit sweater beneath.

She smiled mischievously. "They'll see me coming and that's the way I want it."

"Did you go to the casino last night?"

"Yes indeed, and won ten bucks on the slots."

"How was Oriano's performance?"

"Superb, though I don't approve of his doing that kind of work. It isn't true ballet, you know."

"I know, but he enjoys working."

"And it gave him an excuse to see Tahoe and do the gambling bit."

"Does he gamble?"

"I don't know. I took a nap early, then went over to catch the late show."

"Was the cast there?"

"Everyone except you."

"I'll catch his act later."

"It's well worth seeing. And the girls are beautifully costumed. The dancing, well. . . ." she shrugged. "It's a lot of fast movements, and the show, as you can guess, isn't long. After all, they want the gaming tables patronized."

"That's what it's all about, isn't it?"

"Sure is. Only hope the cast isn't too tired. I'm beginning to get edgy."

"No need to. You have an excellent troupe and they'll work their hearts out for Theodoric."

The ride was brief and when we reached the cabaret, I drove off the road into a tree-shaded area. Most of the cast were seated on the steps, enjoying the morning sunshine. They were bundled up in heavy sweaters, for the air was brisk and not yet warmed by the October sun.

I was just about to get out of the car when I heard the familiar putt-putt of a small engine. I looked in my rear view mirror and saw Oriano with Holly, her arms around his waist, astride a motorbike. I was so startled, I cried out.

Mirabel said, "What is it?"

"Oriano and Holly just came. He rides a motorbike."

"I know, and I'm not keen about it. Especially with the roads around here. If he ever takes a header, we're in for trouble."

"Don't forget Holly," I said. "She could be thrown, too."

Mirabel said, "Not with the grip she's got around his waist." She eased her bulk out of the car. "Holly can ride, too, you know."

"I didn't know."

"Oriano was teaching her yesterday and I must say she did very well."

"You mean," I said, "she could drive it alone?"

"She could and she did. In fact, she took Oriano to the casino and drove back to dress."

"Did she ride it back to the casino?"

"No," Mirabel said. "I saw it outside the motel when I left to go to the casino."

"How did you get there?"

She gave me a puzzled look. "I rented a car last night. What are you getting at?"

"Nothing," I said. "I knew you didn't have transportation and you said you took a nap before you went to see Oriano's performance."

"Well, you can't get around here without a car," she said.

"Was the bike at the motel when you came back?"

Her brow furrowed. "I believe it was. Holly probably got a ride to the casino with the others. What's bothering you, Nicki?"

I wondered if I should mention the motorbike I'd heard, then decided against it. Suspicion would point to Holly—or even Oriano, yet he'd have no motive for doing anything to jeopardize the production.

I said, "Nothing, really. I just think it's risky for Holly to be riding it."

"So do I," Mirabel said. "But I can't forbid her to do it any more than I can Oriano. Now let's get inside." She moved ahead with her brisk stride, calling to Oriano and Holly to come along. I waved to them, but they were still too engrossed in each other to notice that there were others about. Or care, for that matter. It was understandable. They were both young, attractive, and filled with a zest for life. Holly seemed completely infatuated with him; and if he wasn't with her, he was certainly putting on a good act.

Theo, who'd been inside, came to the door, clapped his hands and ordered everyone on stage. Mirabel took him aside and engaged him in an earnest conversation. Once he glanced over at me and from his sober features, I knew Mirabel must be relating what I'd told her about last night.

I continued on to the stage with the others. We

checked the boards and found they'd been nailed down and the first set was already up. It was simple but effective: a gaunt house where the medium lived and carried on her seances. A dreary, grim place, but outside it were flowered paths and a grassy lawn.

We went to our dressing rooms and changed. I'd seen no sign of the broken chair. Everything was in order and a glance upward had revealed the sandbag, no doubt hanging securely on a new rope.

Holly came into the dressing room as I was about to leave. "Oh, Nicki, you should have seen Oriano last night. He was superb."

"Mirabel told me," I said. "I'll catch his show one of these nights."

She giggled. "You have a show of your own with Amorita Davina."

Holly's belittling tone irritated me. "I'm already very fond of her."

"You must be kidding." She pulled off her boots, tossed them beneath her dressing table, and put on her ballet slippers, winding the ribbons firmly about her ankles and tying them securely.

"I'm not kidding," I said firmly. "I like Amorita and she's been very kind to me."

"Maybe I'd like her too if she invited me to live in a castle. But, on second thought, I'd refuse."

I smiled despite myself. "You needn't tell me why."

"Jealous?"

"No," I said. "You and Oriano make a very handsome pair."

She looked pleased. "Our pictures were taken at the casino last night. They will make all the papers."

"Good," I approved. "I hope the ballet will get a mention."

"I suppose it will," she said. "But his press agent asked if I'd mind being referred to as his new romantic interest. I said, 'Why should I when I am?'"

66

"Just don't get hurt. And don't let his press agent use you."

She shrugged. "I can take care of myself."

"I'm sure you can."

"But I was so annoyed," she went on. "Oriano had promised to take me for a drive around the lake after the show."

"On the motorbike?"

"No," she said scornfully. "I made him promise to let me use it while I'm here. I'm talking about his manager. He insisted on Oriano meeting with him after the show. It seems he's had some heavy gambling losses and he's lost more than he'll make at the casino."

I said, "That's tough," and thought, more problems for Mirabel and Theodoric.

Holly tossed her blonde mane of hair to the back and secured it with a ribbon. "He'll make out."

"I hope so," I said. "We'd better get on stage."

EIGHT

The cast, along with Oriano, was already there and Theodoric was expounding on the story.

"As you know, this scene takes place outside the medium's home. The contrast is important, the outside being alive and bright, the inside funereal. Now this is what the audience will see as the curtain rises. Slowly Oriano, as the ghost, will materialize from one of those thickets you see. By a lighting trick he will appear to take form.

"Then, while he waits, Lorraine—that's you, Nicki—emerges from the house. You'll wear a dress of dark green chiffon, a flowing dress, but one which will not make a light spirit of a woman who is supposed to be a medium and deals with spectres. Lorraine sees the ghost, but doesn't know he isn't human, and she is attracted to him."

"How will I be dressed?" Oriano asked.

"Completely in white."

He was pleased. "I look good in white."

Holly said, "What about me?"

"You'll be in white also," Mirabel said. "Flowing chiffon, so that when you preform your pas de deux, the filmy fabric will almost conceal Oriano, making your spirits seem to blend."

Holly pirouetted over to him, circled him, then, still en pointe, paused to face him. His hands lightly enclosed her waist and he kissed her cheek. She made a fetching picture as she held the pose, still on her toes.

"Let's get on with this," Theo said, sounding impatient. "Lorraine is drawn to this stranger and they dance the theme of a new love. The audience, but not they, will see Oriano's ghostly girlfriend materialize. That's you, Holly, and we will surround you with the illusion of being created out of air. The girl ghost watches the pas de deux and is affected by it, saddened to tears and a desire to escape before she sees too much. But ghosts are controlled by forces too, and she cannot escape, so she must reduce her fears and anxieties by means of the dance. Through this, she hopes to draw Oriano away from Lorraine. That's the first scene. There are seven more."

"Should be very effective," Oriano conceded.

"Let's see how effective," Mirabel said. "We've only a piano, but it will have to do. How about the lighting?"

An electrician reported that he'd already tested the apparatus, it worked well, and there should be no trouble materializing the ghosts. We broke ranks and started to limber up. There was no barre, so we used straight-back chairs to support us as we posed and postured, then danced about the stage to further limber our muscles. The piano gave a fanfare of music to draw our attention.

Theo gave the order for us to clear the stage. I went to the rear of the stage and stood where the door of the medium's house would be. The others took their places in the wings to await their cues. The pianist began the music and on cue, I sauntered out of the house as if to enjoy a brief constitutional along one of the paths.

My dress would not be flattering in this scene, though there were some gorgeous costumes for later when I would use my skills and arts to lure Oriano to the land of the living, and away from Holly.

With a start of surprise, I saw him and studied him curiously as I walked lightly and, at first, hesitantly, in his direction. He raised his arms and came toward me. I accepted him at once and we began our pas de deux. We performed well together, neither of us flawing the performance even once. Oriano had perfect control of his body; he was strong and agile. It was a pleasure to dance with him.

Holly had been made to materialize. On cue, Oriano and I separated, and as we did so, a dozen lovely ghosts from the corps de ballet formed a ring around me, keeping me from going back to him. When I tried to break through the circle, they seemed to possess invisible means of preventing me from doing so, and I threw myself again and again at this unseen barrier.

All the while, Holly entreated Oriano, through the dance, to return to her, but he refused, until the circle of ghostly dancers pressed closer and closer to me, preventing him from reaching me. He circled them, attempting through clever steps to outwit them and break through the ring they'd created around me, but each time they prevented him from doing so. Finally, they turned to me and their gestures became menacing, their facial expressions filled with hate. Realizing they would harm me if he persisted in his efforts to reach me, he backed off and turned to Holly.

She began to dance around him. At first, he ignored her, but as the copious folds of the garments she would wear started to enclose him, he came under her spell and they began a pas de deux. Their movements were gentle at first, then gave way to wild abandon, until finally she had lured him to the darker part of the stage which led to their spirit world. Once he was safely under the spell of Katiana—the spirit of a once-famous ballerina, according to the real Lorraine—the ghost dancers abandoned me and danced back to their world. As they did, I followed, arms outstretched, pleading for his return. I danced halfheartedly; then, as hope left me, my arms dropped to my sides, my form became limp, and, as if all life had drained from me, I fell in a faint.

Theo and Mirabel complimented us on some things, corrected us on others, and put us through the scene two more times. In between, Theo had the corps de ballet repeat their ghost dance three times. Then he called Adeline Thornley from the group. She was short and pert, with a mop of black hair cut close to her head so that it was a mass of curls.

Theodoric addressed her. "Miss Rousseau wishes to try a brief pas de deux with you and Oriano. It will be done just after the corps de ballet has discouraged him from attempting to reach Nicki. He is still saddened, but you will distract him with your childlike innocence. He'll forget about his attraction for the worldly creature and will dance with you. How about it, Oriano?"

Oriano came out of the shadowy reaches, regarded Adeline with interest, and nodded approval. "What is your name?" he asked.

"Adeline Thornley," she said.

"I've watched you," Oriano said, his eyes regarding her warmly. "You're pretty good."

Theodoric said, "You, Adeline, and your sisters have been instructed to distract Oriano's attention from the worldly creature he has become infatuated with. Since you are the most beautiful, the other dancers give deference to you by remaining a discreet distance from you, closing in only when Oriano attempts to maneuver his way through the circle you've all made around Lorraine. It takes a while for you to attract his attention, but you finally do."

Theodoric came up on stage then, and with graceful movements and words showed Oriano and Adeline what he wished. He nodded to the pianist, who started the music. Adeline caught the mood immediately. There was nothing lustful about her dance; rather, it had an appealing innocence which was ideal for distracting Oriano's attention from me and causing him to pursue her. There was the merest touch of flirtatiousness to her manner and Oriano responded beautifully. Theo stopped them only once, and then only to tell her when she was to rejoin the corps de ballet who followed at a distance. Holly would move in and she and Oriano would perform their pas de deux—a joyous dance because he had forgotten Lorraine by now and was content to be with the ghostly partner who loved him.

We went through the complete scene then. Adeline was radiant with happiness at having been given a large role, and the second time she performed the dance with Oriano, she was so good that the entire cast broke into applause in which even Theodoric and Mirabel joined. It was a tribute to the girl, whose eyes glistened with tears of gratitude.

Everyone applauded, with the exception of Holly, and her pas de deux with Oriano suffered as a result of her resentment. She had to repeat it twice before Mirabel and Theodoric were satisfied. Even then, Mirabel walked to the foot of the stage and called Holly to come out.

"What's wrong with you?" Mirabel asked.

Holly's eyes flashed angrily. "Nothing. Why?"

"Your dance was wooden. You should be triumphant. One of your handmaidens was successful in luring Oriano from the earth maid."

"Why can't I lure him myself?" Holly protested.

"Because it wouldn't be as effective," Mirabel replied

with an exaggerated quiet, as if she were fast losing patience with Holly.

"I don't agree," Holly said.

Mirabel said, "It happens to be my book, not yours."

"Do you wish to continue in the role?" Theodoric had joined Mirabel, and his voice held the same deadly calm as hers.

"Of course I do." Holly's tone became placating. "It's just that I feel that added dance with Adeline makes Oriano appear fickle."

"Perhaps he is," Theodoric said, giving Holly a meaningful look.

Holly's face flamed. "Would you like me to try it again?"

"Please," Theodoric said. "And remember, the entire cast must perform as a team. Not competitively, but with each member working to perfect his role so as to make the whole pure enchantment."

"I'm sorry," Holly said. "You're right, of course."

Mirabel nodded forgiveness. "Be a good girl now and take your place. We'll start with Adeline, separated slightly from the group so that she attracts Oriano's attention. Don't be too upset, Holly. In a later scene, you'll destroy Adeline, just as you destroy Nicki at the end. Yours is a violently possessive love. But since Adeline is already a spirit, you'll drive her, through the dance, from the rest of your handmaidens."

Theodoric nodded approval. "Excellent, Mirabel. The more conflict, the better we can hold the audience."

I took my place in the center of the stage, the corps de ballet gathered around me, and the pianist started the music. It went smoothly, and if Adeline had been frightened by Holly's outburst, she gave no sign of it. Her dance with Oriano was beautiful. I saw him mouth a few words to her, though his lips scarcely moved. It must have been complimentary, for color flooded her face and her eyes thanked him.

I hoped Holly, from her place in the shadowy reaches of the stage, hadn't noticed. I was beginning to tire, as were other members of the cast, and I feared resentment might show in her dance. But it didn't. She was ready when Oriano joined her, and their dance was as exquisitely beautiful as when he performed with Adeline.

NINE

We were finally excused and retired to our dressing rooms. Holly was tight-lipped, obviously still smarting from the rebuff she'd received from Theodoric. A light knock sounded on our door and I opened it. It was Adeline Thornley. If she was apprehensive, it was hidden well behind the friendly smile she gave me.

Miss Rousseau said I was to share the dressing room with you," she said. "I hope you don't mind."

"Of course not," I said. "There's another dressing table here, so we won't be crowded."

"Thanks," she said. "The room the corps de ballet is using is really jammed. It's going to be something when we have dress rehearsal."

Holly, standing before the full length mirror, eyed us in it without turning. "I suppose sharing this dressing room was your idea."

Adeline said, "I wouldn't be so presumptuous."

"Oh, yeah? You flirted outrageously with Oriano during the pas de deux. *That's* presumptuous."

"It was part of the dance," Adeline protested. "I tried to do my very best."

Holly turned slowly to face Adeline. "Are you trying to move up to my role?"

Adeline stood her ground, regarding Holly thoughtfully. "That isn't what you're really thinking."

"Just what am I thinking?" Holly demanded, taking a step forward.

"That I'm trying to take Oriano away from you." Adeline's calmness commanded my respect. Most members of the corps de ballet would have been terrified.

Holly's smile was deadly. "I know you are. And you're very stupid to think you'll get away with it. Oriano's mine and I serve notice on you and every other girl in the cast."

"Oh, come on, Holly," I broke in. "Nobody wants Oriano. And I think Adeline's dance with him hypos the scene."

"The best part," Holly retorted, "is when she slips back and turns him over to me."

"So he's yours," Adeline said. "I want only to dance with him in the ballet and, believe me, you're not going to deprive me of the privilege. He's the best premier danseur today and I'm honored to dance with him."

Holly's hand came up and struck Adeline hard across the cheek. "Don't be too certain about my not depriving you. After that remark, I'll see to it that you don't dance in the *Ballad of Lorraine*."

The blow had been struck with such force and came as such a surprise, that the makeup box Adeline had been holding had flown out of her hands. It had broken open and its contents were scattered over the floor.

I stepped between the girls and gripped Holly's arms, pushing her back until I had her lodged against the mirror. She struggled, but I held her firmly.

"Let me go," she exclaimed angrily.

"Behave yourself, Holly," I retorted. "And apologize to Adeline for striking her."

"I won't apologize," she retorted, still struggling.

She kicked out, but I expected it and managed to keep beyond her range. I heard the door open and thought it was Adeline making a hasty exit. But a glance in the mirror revealed Mirabel regarding both Holly and me with perplexity.

"What's going on?" she asked.

"Just a little argument," I said, keeping my tone light. I released my hold on Holly, knowing she'd behave while Mirabel was present.

"About what?" Mirabel stepped into the dressing room, closing the door behind her.

"Me." Adeline was squatted on her haunches, picking up the various pieces of makeup which had spilled from the box.

"What about you?" Mirabel persisted.

Adeline stood up. "It's nothing really. Just a misunderstanding."

Mirabel addressed Holly. "Are you still annoyed because I gave Adeline a larger part in the scene? Or is it that you don't want anyone else to dance with Oriano?"

"I don't care who dances with him," Holly answered sharply. "I just don't want anyone else flirting with him."

"I suggest you take that up with Oriano." Mirabel's resentment matched Holly's. "He's an incurable flirt. You know that. The only prima ballerina who hasn't fallen under his spell is Nicki."

"I'm not talking about a prima ballerina," Holly said. "I'm talking about a very minor member of the corps de ballet who thinks her cuteness is just too, too irresistible."

"Holly," Mirabel said patiently, "we're working against time up here. Oriano's run ends in a week. I hope by then we'll be out of here. I have all ten fingers and toes crossed that we'll have the ballet rehearsed to perfection by then. If we ever get caught in a blizzard, we could be here for God knows how long."

"What's that got to do with Oriano or me?"

"Everything, my dear," Mirabel's voice was almost a plea. "I don't want feuds or jealousies—even petty ones. I want complete cooperation between each and every member of the cast. Please make up with Adeline. I'm sure she isn't after Oriano. He's a rascal where women are concerned, and you ought to have sense enough to know it."

"I should resent that," Holly said indignantly.

"You have my permission to do so," Mirabel replied calmly. "In the meantime, please apologize to Adeline. Neither of you will leave this room until I'm assured that if you can't be friends, you'll not be rivals."

"Believe me, Miss Rousseau, and you, Holly," Adeline said quietly, "I'm not interested in Oriano. I'm honored that I've been chosen to dance with him, not only because my role in the ballet has been enlarged, but because he is such a superb dancer."

Mirabel nodded smiling approval and her eyes moved to Holly. "Come on, dear. Get with it."

"All right," Holly conceded. "I lost my temper. I'm sorry, Adeline."

"You do believe me about Oriano, don't you?" Adeline regarded Holly hopefully.

Holly nodded, even managing a smile. "I'm sorry I struck you. I have a terrible temper and I'm very jealous."

Mirabel said, "At least you admit to your weaknesses. I suggest that you try to curb them."

"Don't you think they're a part of talent?" Holly asked, her eyes now holding a hint of mischief.

"I suppose," Mirabel said. "I'm just relieved Nicki keeps hers in check. At least, I've seen no evidence of weakness, and for that I'm grateful. One prima donna in a show is enough."

Holly spoke over her shoulder on her way to the door. "I don't think you like me, Mirabel."

Mirabel chuckled. "Stop sulking. I love you all."

"So long as we give a good performance," Holly persisted. "If we don't, you'd like to slit our throats. You're on edge too, you know. The *Ballad of Lorraine* could make or break you."

"And I could make or break you, kid," Mirabel said. "Don't forget it."

"You never let me." Holly paused after opening the door. "I'm going for a drive with Oriano. What time is rehearsal tomorrow?"

"Nine," Mirabel replied. "And get to bed early tonight. That's an order."

"I'm not a fool," Holly said. "With little curlyhead over there trying to outshine me, I'll make certain I get my rest—and my practice. As for you, Nicki, I still hope you break an arm on the slot machines. Both of mine are sore from the grip you had on me."

The door closed with a slam. Mirabel's face colored with rage as she headed for it, but when her hand closed around the knob, she paused. "What's the use?" she said. "We need her. I don't want to have to replace anyone now. I'm really very pleased with the way the scene went today. We didn't have too many rehearsals in New York and Oriano wasn't with us at all, but of course he's so skilled, he's the least of my worries. I guess I have only one—Holly. She's quite a bundle of temperament."

"Maybe, now that she's had this blowup, she'll settle down," I ventured.

"I hope so," Adeline said. "I don't want any trouble with her."

Mirabel studied the girl carefully. "*Are* you interested in Oriano other than as a dancing partner in the ballet?"

"Absolutely not," Adeline said. "Oh, I'm not denying

he's handsome and certainly knows how to make a girl feel important. But at present, I'm interested in one thing—my role in the *Ballad of Lorraine*. To me, the story is so good it deserves the best I can give it."

Mirabel smiled her gratitude and placed an arm about Adeline's shoulders. "Good girl. I'm glad I chose you. How old are you?"

"Eighteen," Adeline said.

"You look about twelve," Mirabel said.

I nodded my agreement.

"Keep an eye on her," Mirabel directed me. "Her face is still red. That must have been quite a blow Holly struck."

Adeline managed a smile. "I knew I'd been hit."

"I'm glad I came in here," Mirabel said. "Theodoric suggested I do so, after I told Adeline to pick up her things and share the dressing room with you."

I said, "Don't tell me Theodoric's been on the receiving end of Holly's temper."

"He wouldn't take it," Mirabel said. "But he's worked with her in several shows and has seen her behavior with others in the cast."

"I'll watch out for Adeline," I assured Mirabel.

"Good."

"Want a ride back to the motel?" I asked.

"No. Theo is giving me a lift. I did tell you I had a rented car, didn't I?"

"Yes, but I brought you out this morning."

She smiled. "If I get the opportunity to save on gas and mileage, I'll not pass it up. I'm not that affluent."

I laughed. "I'll give you a ride any time."

"I'll remember that. Good-bye, Adeline. If you have any problems with Holly—no matter how minor—come to me. We don't want the show to suffer. If Holly becomes too difficult, we'll replace her—though God knows I don't want to."

After Mirabel left, I helped Adeline pick up the rest

of her makeup, and showed her the table which she would use. She placed some of her things in the narrow drawer and left her slippers beneath the table.

"Like a ride to the motel?" I asked.

"I didn't think you were staying there."

"I'm not, but I'll be happy to take you back."

"Thanks, Nicki, but despite the unpleasantness, I'm so happy about my enlarged part that I'd just like to be by myself for a while and glory in it. Then I'll walk back to the motel and drop my mother a line. She's a widow and has made a lot of sacrifices so that I might devote myself to the ballet. Now she'll know I'm making headway."

"You certainly are. You were terrific today. And I believe the *Ballad of Lorraine* is really going to be a hit."

"Oh, I hope so," she said, her eyes shining. "Thanks."

We left together. She took off in the direction of the lake. I drove directly to the castle.

TEN

I drew up before Castle Morvant and parked alongside the Rolls. As I passed it, on impulse I touched the hood. It was warm, indicating Amorita had only recently returned. She opened the door, called out a warm greeting and motioned me not to come into the house.

"I thought I'd take you for a stroll about the grounds. I'll show you the garage and also my rehearsal room."

"You still dance?"

She looked amused at my surprise. "Indeed, yes. How else could I be so supple at my age?"

We walked around the castle to the rear of the grounds. On our way, I noticed an attractive summer house located in the midst of a rose garden. However, there were few blooms, though the ones left were enormous. The house was a good size, octagonal in shape and furnished with wicker chairs, the seats and backs of which were cushioned with colorful pillows.

We moved past it and proceeded to a building of moderate size with a two-sided roof that slanted from its tip almost to the ground. Amorita took a key from her sweater pocket and opened the door. She motioned me to go in ahead of her. I was momentarily blinded and I thought it was because I'd come from bright sunlight into muted light. But when she snapped on the lights, I noted there were no windows.

I exclaimed aloud in surprise to see one wall mirrored, and before it a barre. The floor was smooth and highly polished.

"How do you like it?" she asked.

"Fantastic," I said. "Will you dance for me?"

"Not today, my dear," she said. She motioned to the corner of the room nearest us. Four chairs circled a round table. "Do sit down and tell me about your day. And before you start, I want you to know this room is available to you whenever you wish to use it."

"Thank you, Amorita," I said. "It's very dear of you."

"No, it isn't." She smiled. "I want to make your visit as pleasant as possible. It so happens I had a little heart-to-heart with my grandnephew this morning. He told me he'd disown me if I didn't do everything to make your stay enjoyable."

My smile was self-conscious. "I wish he hadn't."

She patted my arm reassuringly. "I'm only joking. I did talk with him though. I only hope he's made the impression on you that you've made on him. He's more than fond of you, my dear. I don't expect you to turn cartwheels at the revelation, but do you find him the least bit appealing?"

"He's been very gracious to me," I replied evasively. "What more can I say?"

"I can see I've made you uncomfortable. Forgive me for being so outspoken. Even Steve scolds me for it." She settled back in the chair. "Tell me about today."

I was glad to switch the conversation away from Steve.

83

I enjoyed his attention, his kindness, and the fact that I found being with him more pleasurable than with any other man I'd known. Not that I'd cultivated many. There just wasn't time for it in the ballet. So many hours of practice had to be given to perfecting techniques and to keeping oneself in trim. Besides, I didn't want to fall in love. That could end my career suddenly, for I always felt that when I married I would want to devote my life to my husband and the raising of a family. And I didn't want to retire from dancing yet; I didn't feel I was ready. I believed Amorita would understand, yet I didn't wish to discuss it with her, so I switched to the subject of today's rehearsal.

"I noticed your face shadow a little when you spoke of little Adeline Thornley," she said.

I regarded her curiously. "I didn't say she was little."

"You described the scene and her dancing. I got the picture of a piquant little thing. A combination of youthful innocence and talent."

"That describes her perfectly," I said. "Her part added a great deal to the scene."

"Then why did you look disturbed when you spoke of her?"

I shrugged. "Oh—a little problem came up."

Amorita's head tilted to one side. "Jealousy?"

I nodded. "Holly Larkin—who dances as the ghost from the spirit world and who resents Oriano's interest in Lorraine—my character—thought Adeline put more into the dance with Oriano than was necessary."

"Did she?"

"No."

Amorita's smile was reflective. "It keeps the ballet interesting to have feuds going. I take it Holly is quite temperamental."

"Temperamental with a touch of violence," I said. "She struck Adeline quite a blow."

Amorita nodded knowingly. "That's part of it. I hope Adeline stood up to her."

"Verbally she did very well. As for the other, Adeline is a gentle, soft person. However, I think Holly will let her alone. Theodoric will brook no nonsense. She could lose the part and that she doesn't want. Also, Mirabel told her to behave."

Amorita looked thoughtful. "I have an idea this ballet will not be a dull one."

"If by that you mean feuds, I hope we'll have no more."

"I hope not." Amorita stood up. "I made salads for us. They should be nicely chilled by now. And I almost forgot." Her eyes twinkled mischievously. "Steve phoned, and asked me to tell you that if you're available, he'd like to take you out to dinner."

"May I call his office?"

"To refuse or accept?"

I laughed. "To accept."

"He said that if you should accept, there was no need to call."

"Thank you, Amorita. And I am famished. I'll relish the salad, after which I'd like to rest awhile and then relax in a tub."

"Come along, my dear."

We left the rehearsal room and before we went inside, I garaged my car. Amorita said she'd garage hers later.

When Steve came that night, he asked her if she wanted him to put her car away, but she told him what she'd told me earlier. I wore a long plaid skirt, with matching fringed shawl. A long-sleeved, high turtleneck sweater completed my costume. Even so, Steve used the heater in his car and the warmth felt good.

We had a leisurely dinner at a chalet with a rustic air. It had a combo which was specializing in Cole Porter tunes that night and we danced a little, once I assured Steve I wasn't too tired.

I liked being in his arms. He had an excellent sense of rhythm and gave a strong lead. He even sang the chorus of one of the tunes and I was pleasantly surprised at his baritone voice.

Outside again, he said, "Would a drive around the lake bore you?"

"I'd call it a perfect ending to a very happy evening."

"I'm glad," he said. "I want to please you, Nicki. I more than like you, you know, but I have a feeling you don't want to become involved."

"This afternoon I'd have assured you you were correct," I told him honestly. "Tonight—well, it could be moon magic except there's no moon. So . . . ."

"Go on," he urged.

"It has to be you," I said.

His arms moved to enclose my waist, but I stepped back and my shoes made crunching sounds on the gravel driveway. "Not yet. I honestly don't know if I do want to become involved. And I *must* know, before I even let you kiss me."

He nodded. "I want you to know. I've never proposed to a girl before and I want to propose to you even before I've kissed you. But I won't."

"Thanks—both for your consideration and your patience."

He did kiss me though, on the cheek. Then he opened the car door for me and held it while I got in. Before he started the motor, he excused himself and used his car phone to check with his answering service.

He listened a few moments, then smiled patiently and said, "Okay, Bess, put her on." After a pause, he said, "Hello, Eleanor. What seems to be the trouble? . . . . Yes, I am gallivanting . . . . Who with? A very lovely girl . . . . Of course I mind your interfering since it's my night off, but since you're my patient and a very demanding one, there isn't much I can do about it. What's your problem? . . . . Another one of those headaches? When did it start? . . . . Have you been taking the red capsules I gave you? . . . . I didn't think so. If you had, you wouldn't be suffering. Take one. . . . Of course, immediately, and another before you go to bed. Tomorrow get back on schedule. I'll drop by in the morning. Don't worry, you're in good shape. *If* you take the medicine as I've directed on the label."

He hung up and grinned tolerantly. "High blood pressure, a lot of years, and an obstinacy about taking medicine. Wrap it up and that's Eleanor."

The phone buzzed again. He made a gesture of helplessness. This time I handed him the phone. He spoke very little, listened a great deal, then hung up and started the car.

"Among other things, I'm the medical examiner here. A girl's body was just taken from the lake—the south end. I've got to go there. Hang on! I can legally break speed laws on medical examiner business."

The car took curves well, bumped over the rougher parts of the road, and roared at sixty-five before we reached the south end of the lake. It was a wonder to me how Steve managed, considering the narrow, winding road.

A Nevada state trooper directed us to the far end of a marina. There, on the dock, under a tarpaulin, was a grim outline. Steve stepped out of the car.

"Stay here," he said. "I won't be long."

ELEVEN

I watched him move rapidly along the dock until he reached the covered form. He bent forward, raised the tarp, then knelt—and while a trooper held a flashlight on the body, he made a brief examination. Then he covered the body, stood up, and turned to the three troopers whom he engaged in conversation. He also talked to a small group of people who had apparently found the body. With a final word to the troopers, he walked briskly back to the car, but he didn't get in.

"Do you have the stamina to look at the body?"

I was too stunned at his question to reply.

"I know it's a lot to ask, Nicki, but I noticed the legs of this girl seem to be those of a dancer. The muscles are well developed. And the trooper found a silver pin fastened to her blouse. Its design is that of a ballet dancer en pointe, I believe you'd say. I think that means on her toes?"

"That's right, Steve," I said nervously. "But I hope it's no one from the ballet."

"So do I," he said. "And if you don't want to look, it's okay. But there's no other identification on her. And that pin really isn't identification, except that with you here rehearsing a ballet, I thought maybe . . . ." His voice trailed off.

"I'll look."

He held my elbow lightly as he guided me along the dock to the covered form. He signaled to the trooper with the flash, who raised the tarp and threw the beam of the flashlight on a pallid, composed face.

I screamed once, then covered my mouth as I turned away. "It's—it's Adeline Thornley. She was a member of our company."

Steve passed on that information to one of the troopers, then took me back to the car, and studied me in the light of the dash.

"I'm terribly sorry," he said. "Did you know her well?"

"No. This is her first time in any ballet I've been in. Theo will know where she comes from and whom to notify. She was very talented," I added, as if that made any difference.

"I just gave them Theodoric's name and informed them the troupe is at the Spindle Motel."

"What could have happened? She was fully dressed."

"There are no witnesses as to just what happened. It will have to wait until I do a postmortem tomorrow."

I frowned. "I can't believe she slipped and fell. A ballet dancer has an excellent sense of balance."

"What *do* you believe?"

The sternness of his tone startled me.

"Nothing, really." I lowered my eyes and studied my hands, clasped tightly in my lap.

Steve's hand covered them. "Come on, Nicki. Tell me. As you say, a ballet dancer has an excellent sense of balance. Adeline didn't slip and strike her head, rendering her unconscious. I doubt we'll find water in her lungs."

"What are *you* saying," I asked.

"That she was murdered."

"Oh, Steve. Are you certain?"

He nodded. "Pretty sure. There are marks around her throat. I'll do the postmortem. In the meantime, we'll treat it as if it were an accident."

I nodded, but I felt sick inside, remembering what Holly had said to Adeline. I covered my face with my hands and moaned in anguish.

Steve's arm encircled my shoulders. "Please tell me."

I lowered my hands, but I still couldn't look into his eyes. I knew I'd have to tell him, yet I couldn't believe that Holly was guilty of such a horrible act.

"This afternoon," I said, "Holly Larkin and Adeline Thornley had a disagreement. I can't say Adeline quarreled with Holly, but she stood up to her."

"What about?"

"Oriano—the male lead. Holly is quite overwhelmed by the attention he's showing her, and was afraid Adeline was moving in."

"Was she?"

"I'm certain she wasn't and she told Holly so."

"What started the feud, or quarrel, or argument or whatever?"

"Mirabel wanted a little more conflict in the first scene and decided to have Adeline, who was a member of the corps de ballet, slip from the group and do a pas de deux with Oriano. You saw Adeline. Oriano was quite impressed."

He nodded.

"Oriano and she danced beautifully together. Holly became angry and made a scene on stage. Mirabel called her on it and Theodoric asked Holly if she'd like to be replaced. That calmed her, until she learned Adeline was to share our dressing room. As I think back,

I believe Holly may have suspected that Mirabel put Adeline in with us deliberately to needle her."

"Are you of that?"

"No. There aren't enough dressing rooms in the cabaret and I know the corps de ballet must be terribly jammed in the one room. Also, I thought it only fair that, since Adeline's role was enlarged, she should share our room. There was plenty of space for her."

"Isn't the prima ballerina supposed to have a dressing room to herself?"

"Yes. But it's nothing to make an issue of."

"Thank God you don't have temperament."

"Oh, I have," I assured him. "But not over something so petty."

"Do you suspect Holly might have had something to do with Adeline's death?"

"I hope not."

"What did she say that made you think of her?"

"She said she'd see to it that Adeline never performed in the *Ballad of Lorraine*."

Steve's brows raised laconically. "She may live to rue the day."

"But she apologized afterward."

"After what?" Steve countered.

"Well, she struck Adeline across the face with her open palm. I got between the girls and grabbed Holly. Mirabel came in while I was still trying to cope with Holly and ordered her to apologize."

"Let's go see Holly." Steve backed the car and headed for the road. "Don't say anything about its being murder. If the troopers don't get there before us, Holly won't know anything about it, and if she is guilty, she might reveal it."

I said, "I feel low and sneaky doing a thing like this."

His eyes rebuked me. "Have you forgotten that girl lying out there on the dock?"

"I'm sorry. For a moment I did. She had an enchanting way about her. It came through in the brief pas de deux she did with Oriano. I left the rehearsal with her and offered her a ride back to the Spindle. She refused; she wanted to take a stroll along the lake. She was so happy about her wonderful break that she wanted to be alone. Then she was going back and write her mother. Adeline told me her mother was widowed and had made many sacrifices to enable her to study ballet."

"I wish she'd accepted the ride back with you."

"So do I. She'd probably be alive now."

"No telling. I'll have to inform the troopers of what you told me. They'll check with everyone regarding their whereabouts, and also if anyone saw Adeline after rehearsal. She may have returned to the motel and written that letter."

"I wonder," I said.

"What do you mean?"

"Well, you know there are a lot of kooky characters with warped minds around today. Someone like that might have killed her."

"This is the second girl's body that's been taken from the water," Steve mused.

I nodded. "The other incident was in California, wasn't it?"

He nodded, but made no further comment, devoting his attention to driving. He drove into one of the parking slots in front of the motel, just as Holly pulled in on the motorbike. The putt-putt of the motor sounded like the one I'd heard start up and drive away from Castle Morvant. I knew I'd have to tell Steve about it, knowing it would weave a web of suspicion more tightly around Holly. I had no idea just how much more tightly, until I got out of the car and noticed her boots were caked with dried mud.

She greeted me cheerily, giving no hint of the fact that she didn't care particularly about me. From the way she observed Steve, it was obvious he met with her approval.

She said, "Better not let Mirabel see you. She gave orders at the cabaret that everyone was to get to bed early."

I pointed to her boots. "You look as if you took a spill."

She laughed. "I slipped partially into the water. I was walking near the edge and slipped on some wet grass."

I said, "This is Dr. Steve Fenmore, Amorita Davina's grandnephew. I've already told him about you."

She acknowledged the introduction and eyed me guardedly. "Just what did you tell him?"

I ignored the question. "Adeline's body was taken from the lake a short time ago."

"What?" If Holly was feigning, she was doing a superb job.

"You heard me," I said. "Did you see her after rehearsal?"

She shook her head dazedly. "Oriano was to take me for a ride, but he had to cancel out because of a meeting with his debtors."

"Did you take a ride around the lake?" Steve asked.

She eyed him speculatively. "Why?"

"I was wondering if you might have seen Adeline. Maybe she slipped in, too."

"Just what is your interest in Adeline?" Holly asked.

"I'm the medical examiner here," Steve said.

"That still doesn't give you the right to cross-examine me."

"No," he agreed. "But the police will."

"After informing me of my rights," she said tersely. "Excuse me."

She turned abruptly and went inside. Steve and I exchanged glances and followed. She was waiting for us inside the door. "You might check with Mirabel. I passed her on the bike. She was driving toward the motel."

"When?" Steve asked.

"A short time ago," Holly said. "Now excuse me. I doubt I'll get any rest, but I want to get these muddy boots off. The rest of me isn't very clean either."

In the neon-lit lobby, the caked mud was visible over most of Holly's back. She had indeed taken a fall.

"Are you hurt?" I asked.

"No. I didn't fall hard. Once I knew I couldn't prevent the fall, I just went with it."

She waved a farewell, moved along the hallway, and went to her room. I guided Steve along the corridor, around a corner, and down to the end of the hall where Mirabel's room was located.

I tapped on the door. I heard footsteps approach and Mirabel opened it. She was in the process of putting up her hair and held a roller in her hand.

"Mirabel, this is Steve Fenmore, Amorita's grand-nephew."

She extended a free hand and gripped Steve's firmly. "Your aunt told us about you yesterday when we were up there."

"We have bad news," I said bluntly. "Adeline Thornley drowned in the lake."

She stood there in absolute silence a moment. Her eyes flicked from me to Steve, then back to me. "Are you sure?"

Steve said, "Nicki made a positive identification."

"Oh, my God." Mirabel's large form drooped. "The poor girl. What could have happened?"

"No one knows," Steve said. "Her body has just been recovered from the lake. We came directly here."

"Come in, please." Mirabel stepped back from the door. "Sit where you can. These rooms weren't meant to receive guests."

"I can't stay," Steve said. We remained standing.

"Nicki can't either," Mirabel said. "She's got to get her rest. If the police will let us. Oh, my God. What happened?"

"We don't know," Steve said. "I'm the medical examiner, so I'll perform the autopsy."

Mirabel's head moved forlornly from side to side. "Such a dear girl. A child, really. It just doesn't make sense."

"The state troopers will be here shortly. They'll want to know whom to notify."

"Theodoric has the names and addresses of the cast. He'll give them whatever information they want."

"You probably won't be bothered," Steve said, "unless we find evidence of foul play."

"Oh, God, not that," Mirabel exclaimed. "Who'd destroy someone as gentle and lovely as Adeline?"

"Is Theodoric here?" Steve asked.

"He hasn't been," Mirabel said. "I called his room a few minutes ago and got no answer. Maybe he's come back since."

"I'll check," I said. "He'll have to know."

"He's at the other end of the corridor," Mirabel said. "It's going to hit him hard. He favored Adeline. Her youth, beauty, and talent. And she meets with an accident."

"We don't know that it was an accident," Steve said. "We're assuming it was."

"I'm beginning to wonder if the *Ballad of Lorraine* is jinxed." Mirabel addressed her remark to me.

I knew what she meant, but made no answer. I was beginning to wonder the same thing. Only *I* wondered who was behind it. Who didn't want the ballad produced? An enemy of Mirabel's? Or one of Theodoric's? Or perhaps an avowed enemy of contemporary ballet—and that pointed directly to Amorita.

Steve raised a forefinger as a sudden thought occurred to him. "Oh, there is a question I would like to ask you, Miss Rousseau."

"Make it Mirabel. I don't go for the formal stuff."

"Thanks, Mirabel. We talked with Holly downstairs. She pulled in on the motorbike just as we did."

"You mean she's driving that damned machine?" Mirabel exclaimed, half in exasperation, half in anger.

Steve smiled. "Did you forbid her to?"

"I can't do that," she replied. "But I talked with her today about it. I asked her not to ride it. She's not even supposed to be out." She favored me with a glance. "Nor are you, my dear. The fact that Steve happens to be Amorita's kin doesn't give you special privileges."

"I know, Mirabel," I said. "And I'd have been back to the castle earlier, but Steve got the call to come to the dock."

She looked reflective. "So that's how you knew about Adeline."

Steve said, "Holly told us she saw you tonight."

Mirabel looked blank. "Tonight?"

Steve nodded. "Were you riding or walking?"

"I wasn't out tonight. I had room service send my dinner up, and I put my tray outside when I finished. Why should she say such a thing?"

"She must have been mistaken," I said.

"I doubt anyone would mistake me for someone else," Mirabel said. "Not with the clothes I wear."

"They wouldn't show up in the dark," Steve said.

"Mine would," Mirabel said emphatically. "Wouldn't they, Nicki?"

I smiled. "Mirabel deliberately chooses clothes that will call attention to her."

She frowned, then suddenly said, "Why would Holly make such a statement?"

"She said you were driving toward the motel," I explained. "Apparently she was going in the opposite direction."

"I wasn't driving in *any* direction," Mirabel said. "I'm doing some rewriting on *Lorraine*. I was doing it with Adeline in mind. Now we'll have to select someone else."

Steve said, "I must bring Nicki back to the castle,

and since we want to see Mr. Coubet, we'll have to move on."

After Mirabel closed the door behind us and we were beyond hearing distance, I said, "I wonder why Holly would say she saw Mirabel if she didn't?"

Steve's smile was grim. "I don't know, unless she wanted to throw suspicion on her."

"I can't believe Holly would kill Adeline. She might make a death wish—she might even make it regarding me—but to actually kill—no."

"Well," Steve said, "it will be something for the police to figure out. Certainly one of them's lying."

We knocked on Theodoric's door, but there was no answer. We returned to the lobby where Steve used the house phone and asked for Theodoric's room by number. The phone rang and rang. He finally hung up.

"I'm taking you back to the castle," he said. "Though I'd prefer that you remain here."

"Why?"

"I have a feeling you'd be safer."

"That's debatable," I said.

"Maybe," he agreed. "Holly is a very aggressive person. And an ambitious one."

"Very," I said. He gave me an odd look and I nodded. "She'd like me to break an arm on the slots. That's what she said."

"Don't let me see you near one," he warned. "She might plant an explosive to go off when you deposit the coin."

"Seriously," I said, "I'm more inclined to think that if Adeline did meet with foul play, it was at the hands of someone who doesn't want Mirabel's ballet to be produced."

"Let's get back to the car. Since you insist on staying at the castle, I'll take you there, then come back. I'll have to repeat what I've learned about Holly to the troopers."

"They can check it with the cast and Mirabel," I said.

"And Theodoric," Steve remarked thoughtfully. "I wonder where he is."

"I haven't the faintest idea."

"I'm wondering if you were meant to be a victim and when you seemed to have nine lives, the murderer turned to someone less alert."

"You mean, you think if it was murder, it's someone connected with the ballet?"

"I'm pretty sure it *was* murder," Steve said quietly. "And yes, I'm inclined to think it was someone connected with the ballet."

"I didn't mention his aunt's overwhelming interest in the ballet. We were both rather silent as we drove through the dark to Castle Morvant.

TWELVE

Steve unlocked the door of the castle and we found Amorita seated before a glowing fireplace. She was dozing, but woke up instantly. Steve told her the whole story about the death of Adeline, even the fact that it was apparently murder.

"The poor child," Amorita said. "Could she have been the victim of some of those awful characters I've seen around the lake the last three or four years?"

"Possibly," Steve said.

"They look as if they're capable of anything, including murder. And you may recall, another girl was taken from the lake only a few months ago. I'm extremely sorry this happened. For the poor girl mostly, of course, but my sympathies also go out to you, Nicki, and to the entire company."

"Thank you," I said.

Amorita sat up very straight and her dark eyes glittered in the glow of the fireplace embers. "This ballet has had more than its share of bad luck. It's a story of violence and murder anyway. It won't have a chance."

"I don't see why not," I said defensively.

"I've seen other ballets beset by bad luck and they either didn't get off the ground or were a miserable failure when performed. The *Ballad of Lorraine* will be no different. Mirabel should forget it."

"I don't agree with you," I said.

"You're talking nonsense and superstition," Steve derided. "In my opinion, when the news gets out, the ballet will be more popular than it may have a right to be."

"I have never known of a ballet, plagued by bad luck, that amounted to anything," Amorita repeated. "I've seen these things happen before. I'm an old has-been, but I'm not senile and my memory is clear. The whole theme of the ballet is evil."

"You don't like modern ballet," Steve reminded her.

"That may be so," Amorita said, half in anger. "I grew up in a different world. I've seen and experienced the better things and I haven't forgotten. Rhythm and grace, and beauty of costume and movement are all important. I admit I don't like modern ballet—it's too earthy—and if there were some means by which I could destroy it, I would."

"Please," I said, "don't judge the *Ballad of Lorraine* before you see some of it. Everything about it is beautiful."

"Do you call the murder of this poor child beautiful?" she demanded harshly.

"You're being unfair," Steve broke in.

"Maybe it's because I'm worried."

"Amorita, come to rehearsal in a day or two, after we've perfected parts of the dance," I urged. "You'll see for yourself. Maybe a dress rehearsal. You'll be convinced that our costumes are as lovely as those in *Giselle* or any other ballet you care to name."

"I'll be there," she said grimly. "You have only to let me know the day and time."

Steve arose. "Good. Now, if I can be sure you two ladies won't start quarreling, I'll go home for a night's sleep. Tomorrow's a busy day for me."

Amorita laughed. "I can assure you I hold Nicki in as high regard as you, my foolish nephew."

"Why foolish?" I asked, happy that our conversation had at last become light in tone.

"Because he hasn't asked you to marry him. I'm not as old-fashioned in matters of love as I am about ballet. He's known you two days. That's sufficient in these modern times."

"She knows how I feel about her. I just haven't persuaded her yet."

"The dance is all-consuming," Amorita said wisely. She waved an arm imperiously at Steve. "Go home. You have our permission."

He gave her an affectionate kiss on the cheek and waved a farewell to me. I felt my color rise at the warmth of his glance and my heartbeat quickened. I was glad his aunt was present. I might not have been so unwavering.

After he departed, Amorita said, "I hope Mirabel cancels the ballet."

"Oh no," I exclaimed.

"Oh yes. Since you came here, there have been many mishaps. I haven't forgotten what almost happened to you. They were narrow escapes. I warned Theodoric that I'll hold him responsible for your safety."

"I wonder where he is tonight," I said.

"Surely you don't suspect him," she exclaimed indignantly.

"I don't want to suspect anyone," I said. "But someone killed Adeline."

"Probably no one connected with the ballet. Her part was minor."

We sat there silently for a moment, trying to believe that. Amorita gave up first.

"Yours isn't." She stabbed the air with a forefinger. "You're the prima ballerina. Have you forgotten the sandbag, the loose boards on the stage, the fur-storage closet upstairs?"

"Then you do believe I was locked in there."

"If you say you were locked in, I belive you."

I suddenly remembered I'd forgotten to tell Steve about the sound of the motorbike the night I was locked in the closet. It would keep. But I'd have to tell it. Certainly, it wouldn't endear me to Holly.

"Go to bed, child," Amorita said. "You're tense and that's not good for a ballet dancer."

"I *am* tired," I said, rising. "Just as soon as Steve has completed the postmortem on Adeline Thornley, I must write her mother."

"Do you know the woman?"

"No. But I can imagine her heartache. A letter might help ease it. If not now, then later. Good night, Amorita."

"Good night, my dear. I'm going to sit here awhile longer."

Once upstairs, I lost no time undressing and getting to bed. I was weary, yet I couldn't sleep. I must have tossed for an hour before deciding I could endure it no longer. I threw the blankets aside, put on my woolen robe and was about to go downstairs, when I heard the wheels of a car crunch along the drive. I went to the window and saw Amorita's Rolls Royce move slowly along the drive until it turned onto the road. I thought I could detect two figures in the front seat, but I wasn't sure.

I went to my door, opened it, and moved cautiously across the corridor to Amorita's room. I opened the door stealthily. I could see her form outlined in the bed. I listened for her breathing, but couldn't detect it. I moved further into the room and boldly flashed on the light switch. There was no need for me to go to the bed. Pillows had been placed the length of the bed to simulate her body.

I turned off the light, returned to my room, locked my door, and got into bed. I lay there until the car returned. I heard it, but I didn't hear Amorita come up the stairs. Only the lightest sound of my knob turning, followed by her door closing, reached my ears.

What sort of game was she playing, I wondered. And why? Should I tell Steve? The murder of a young girl was involved. Certainly, Amorita was up to something. Did she wish to harm me? Had she killed Adeline? I wished Steve hadn't told her that Adeline's death was murder. He hadn't told Mirabel or Holly, and he'd warned me to pretend it was believed to be an accidental drowning.

I was plagued by questions until the gray light of dawn streaked the room. Only then did I relax; I was exhausted and spent, both mentally and physically. I doubted I'd do well at rehearsal and both Mirabel and Theodoric would be piqued. I only hoped they'd be understanding, attributing it to Adeline's untimely death. But it was Amorita who had really robbed me of my sleep, for it was she who didn't want the *Ballad of Lorraine* to be performed.

THIRTEEN

Mirabel and Theodoric were seated at their usual table in the cabaret. The other members of the cast were on the stage. A few were going through the motions of practicing, yet there seemed a listlessness about their work. The piano player, a cigarette dangling from his lips, idly ran his fingers over the keys, improvising mostly. Oriano stood alongside the instrument, his arms on the top of the upright, his head resting on his arms. Obviously, the entire cast was affected by Adeline's death, for an air of gloom pervaded the place. Without even asking, I knew they'd been informed she'd been found in the lake.

I joined Mirabel and Theodoric at the table. I was no sooner seated than Mirabel said, "Adeline was murdered. Strangled."

I thought of the piece of rope which had dangled from the sandbag. "With what?" I asked.

"There was nothing around her neck at the time, but they think probably with a scarf."

Theodoric said, "Who would do such a thing?"

Mirabel said, "I guess we're all suspect."

I glanced up at the stage. "Where's Holly?"

"Sulking in her dressing room," Mirabel said.

I frowned. "Sulking?"

"She's angry with me because I said she couldn't have seen me on the road heading back to the motel. How could she when I hadn't been out? Also, she and Oriano had a disagreement."

Theodoric motioned toward the stage. "From the way they're acting, I think we should call off the rehearsal."

"We can't," Mirabel protested. "We're working against time. Now you'll have to place another girl in Adeline's role."

He was studying the girls on the stage. "I'm thinking of Phyllis Grant."

Mirabel nodded approval. "An excellent choice."

"Since you know Adeline was murdered," I said, "you've undoubtedly been questioned by the police."

"We certainly have," Theodoric said. "You can see the effect it's had on the cast."

"Was everyone alibied?" I asked.

"Most of them went directly to the Spindle from rehearsal," Mirabel said. "Fortunately, they have no money for gambling."

"The only ones who weren't alibied were Holly and Oriano. He claims he was in his room. She says she was riding all over on the motorbike, which bodes ill for her."

"When was Adeline supposed to have been murdered?"

"Around eight." Theodoric supplied the information. "I was dining with Amorita again, so I'm alibied."

My brows raised in surprise. "She didn't tell me."

Theodoric chuckled. "She's always been quite secretive. One knows little about her life. But then, you live quietly also, Nicki."

"I'm devoted to my work," I said. "Did the police notify Adeline's mother?"

Theodoric said, "I gave them her address."

"I wonder if there's enough money for funeral expenses," I said.

Theodoric said, "I talked with Amorita this morning. She told me she had already called Mrs. Thornley and will assume all funeral expenses, including shipment of the body back east."

"How good of her," I said.

Mirabel explained, "Amorita was quite impressed with Adeline's performance yesterday."

"Amorita was here?" I exclaimed.

"Certainly," Theodoric said. "She was watching from just inside the door. If I hadn't turned around and caught a glimpse of her, I'd not have known. I went back and stood with her for a while and we discussed the ballet, after which I invited her to dinner. She slipped out then, saying she'd pick me up at seven, which she did."

I said, "You must have made quite an evening of it."

"No," he replied. "I wished to choreograph some new steps, so our dinner took no more than an hour. We didn't even order cocktails."

"Did she bring you back here?" I asked.

Theodoric gave me an odd look. "Are you cross-examining me?"

I managed a laugh. "No. This just seems like a spooky place at night. I can't imagine your wanting to come here."

"I'm sure it is," he said. "After what happened to Adeline, I don't think I'd care to come here in the evening."

"We've warned the cast against strolling along the lake after dark," Mirabel said. "Incidentally, your doctor said you were the last person known to have seen Adeline alive."

"He's not my doctor," I told her pointedly. "As for being the last person to see her, that's hardly true."

Theodoric nodded agreement. "The last person to see her was the one who murdered her."

"I didn't mean it that way," Mirabel said. "I was just wondering if she might have been going to meet someone. She might have struck up an acquaintance with a young man who could have seemed respectable, yet who could be a maniac."

"It's possible," I said. I was thinking of Amorita's urging me to tell her about Adeline. I remembered her referring to Adeline Thornley as being little before I'd described her. I'd even called her on it, but she dismissed it lightly, stating she'd gotten that impression from my description of her dancing. Yet she'd been here and had observed the girl. I also thought of seeing Amorita's car drive away from the castle. She had had a passenger. Who? Theodoric? Certainly not Steve.

"Honey," Mirabel broke into my musings, "will you please go to the dressing room and see if you can bring Holly out of her sulk?"

"I think you'd have more luck than I."

Mirabel sighed impatiently. "Perhaps ordinarily. But not today."

"Why not?"

"After you and Steve left last night," she said, "I went to her room. I was disturbed by her saying she'd seen me when I was nowhere near the lake. She was a while opening her door. When she did, she was wearing a robe. But her boots were on the floor. They were very muddy. Her clothes were thrown onto a chair, and they, too, were covered with caked mud. I pointed it out to her and she became enraged. Doesn't that seem strange to you?"

"How do you mean?"

"Adeline was murdered," Mirabel exclaimed.

"But no one knew it at that time," I argued.

"Exactly." Mirabel slammed the open palm of her hand on the table. "Exactly. So why should she become enraged?"

"How did she explain the mud?"

"She told me she took a spill. I told her if I caught her on the motorbike once more, I'd have Theodoric dismiss her from the cast. We have to make one replacement now. That isn't so difficult since we only added Adeline's new part yesterday. But Holly rehearsed with Theodoric in New York, just as you did, and we can't afford to lose our leads."

"You're right, of course," I said. "I'll see if I can convince her to come up for rehearsal."

Theodoric excused himself and went to the stage, where he called Phyllis Grant from a group of somber-faced girls. I saw her face light up as he spoke to her. Apparently, she had no qualms about replacing a girl who'd been murdered. I was glad she wasn't superstitious.

Theodoric motioned to the piano player to begin. Oriano bestirred himself and the two started to dance. Theodoric nodded with delight and well he should have, because Phyllis knew the steps and performed well with Oriano. But I could see that Oriano had been deeply affected by Adeline's death. His steps were wooden, his body lacked the easy grace so characteristic of his dancing. For the first time, I wondered if the ballet might be jinxed. But I quickly shrugged off my apprehension. It was Amorita who had implanted the idea in my mind. And perhaps, I thought bitterly, she had a motive for doing so. I thought of her turning the knob of my door last night . . . *why?* I wondered if she suspected I was aware she had left the castle. If not, she soon would be, for I had every intention of telling Steve.

Holly was seated in a straight-back chair before her

dressing table. Her arms rested on the table and her head was bent forward. When I entered, she lifted her eyes to my reflection in the mirror, then lowered her head again.

I sat down and took off my shoes, donning my dancing slippers. "Rehearsal is about to begin," I told her.

"That Mirabel," she exclaimed angrily. "I'd like to kill her."

"Holly, don't say that after what's happened."

She swiveled about so she faced me. "I can't help it. Mirabel saw my muddy clothes last night and because Adeline was found in the lake, she acts as if I strangled her and threw her in."

"I'm sure she doesn't believe that."

"She does and maybe you do, too."

"No," I said. "But why did you tell me you slipped and fell near the water?"

She shrugged. "I thought you'd tell Mirabel if you knew I'd taken a spill off the motorbike. That's what did happen, you know. Right into a mud puddle. In fact, that's what caused the spill. I was going pretty fast and my wheels skidded when they hit the mud."

"I hope you won't ride the bike again," I said.

"Don't worry. Until Adeline's murder is solved, I'm going to sit where I can be seen. And that will be at the motel with the rest of the troupe."

"What about Oriano?" I asked, more to lift her spirits than anything.

"What about him?" she countered.

"I thought he was quite smitten with you."

Her eyes flared angrily. "You mean it the other way around, don't you?"

"No, I don't. And if you'll excuse me, I'll get out of here. I'm not in the mood for quarreling."

She reached out and caught my wrist. "I'm sorry. It's just that everything seems to be going wrong. Oriano and

I quarreled and I'm taking it out on everyone. I'll be good."

"He looks very unhappy," I said. "Phyllis Grant has been selected to take Adeline's part. They're rehearsing now. She's good, but Oriano doesn't feel the dance this morning. Maybe he's unhappy about the quarrel."

"I'd like to think it was that," she said, "but it isn't."

"Want to talk about it?"

"Not much to talk about. We quarreled yesterday. I told a lie last night when I said he couldn't see me because he had to have a meeting regarding his gambling debts. He drove off without me yesterday—told me where I could go."

"Why?"

"He was angry with me for making a scene about Adeline. He was right. I was jealous, and he told me that's something he won't tolerate. He said no woman is going to own him. He told me I could use his motorbike, but he wouldn't see me again outside of rehearsals. Then he walked away, leaving me the motorbike."

"I'm sorry, Holly."

"It's just as well," she said. "Only like a fool, I drove all over yesterday, trying to find him. I went to the casino. He wasn't there. His car wasn't, either. I made the tour around the lake searching for him. I wanted to apologize and"—her eyes held a trace of defiance—"yes, I wanted to ingratiate myself. I hoped he'd forgive me and we could be friends again. I mean it. I know he doesn't want to be tied down. I also know it's important to be seen with him. I'm ambitious and I can always swallow my pride so long as it will advance me."

"Do you still feel that way?"

"Yes, but not about Oriano. Not that I like him less, but I know Adeline's murder affected him deeply. Besides, he could be as worried as I. Neither of us has an alibi."

"Neither has Mirabel, for that matter," I said. "She

was in her room, but no one saw her there until I visited her."

"What about Theodoric?" she asked. "Strange how he picks Adeline out of the corps de ballet, and that same night she's found murdered."

"He had dinner with Amorita Davina, so I guess he's alibied."

"She's a weird one," Holly said.

I thought so too, but wasn't going to admit it. "No, she isn't. She just thinks differently about the ballet. Also, she's lived alone for a long time. That tends to make a person a little strange—or seem so to others."

"She gives me the creeps. I mean, she looks at me and I feel she can read what I'm thinking."

"I'm sure you're wrong," I said. "Let's go upstairs. Mirabel wants to get the rehearsal started."

Holly sighed, tied her blonde hair back with a ribbon, and we left the dressing room. On our way to the stage, she said, "I don't have too much faith in this ballet anymore."

"I hope you're not superstitious."

"No. I'm realistic. I think it's jinxed. Mirabel thinks the same thing and she's plenty worried. I don't blame her. It's her big chance. It's also mine," she added. "I'd like to think I'm wrong about it."

"I'm sure you are." I spoke with more conviction than I felt. I wasn't superstitious either, but I was uneasy about the way things were going. I felt certain Amorita played a large part in the mystery, but I couldn't figure out how.

It turned into a strenuous rehearsal. Phyllis did well, but the rest of us, including Oriano, were too filled with the tragedy of the night before. Theodoric interrupted us several times and made us repeat the steps over and over. Oriano made the most errors. He just couldn't seem to slip into the rhythm of the dance.

However, by the time we went into the last rehearsal

of the scene, he was perfect. All of a sudden the mantle of gloom and despair was lifted and the entire company began to dance as if they enjoyed it. But during rest breaks, Oriano isolated himself. He looked dispirited and miserable. I joined him.

His smile was bitter. "I'm not a very good partner today, am I?"

"What happened to Adeline has had its effect on all of us," I told him.

"I seem to be the worst," he said. "She was a dear girl, a beautiful dancer, and you will probably laugh at this—she touched my heart."

I regarded him with surprise. "What are you saying?"

"I fell in love with her." He nodded at my look of disbelief. "It's true. The moment my arms enclosed her in our pas de deux, I thought—this is the girl for me."

My eyes chided him gently. "Haven't you thought that about other girls, Oriano?"

He smiled mirthlessly. "Not in the same way. Oh—I'm a playboy. I admit it. But Adeline . . ."—his hand touched his heart—"I never felt it like that before and I never hurt inside before."

"Perhaps if you wrote to Adeline's mother and told her," I said. "It might ease her loss."

He seemed to like the idea. "Do you have her address?"

"No. But I'll get it from Theodoric. I'm going to write to Mrs. Thornley."

"You know," he said thoughtfully, "there's gypsy blood in my background, which means I'm superstitious. And I feel this ballet isn't good for any of us. For the first time, I encounter love—deep, real love—and it is instantly snatched from me. It's as if I'm cursed and so is everyone in this ballet."

"I can sympathize with you, Oriano. We've all been deeply affected by what happened to Adeline, but we have to go on. You know that. Don't you think she'd want us to?"

He nodded. "Thanks for being so understanding."

"This ballet is going to make history. It's going to become a standard. It has everything it takes for that."

"It's a morbid damn thing."

"No. Only the crime it's based on. The story is solid."

"So is the earth they pack down on you," Oriano said bitterly. "Of course, you're right. If I didn't have faith in it, I shouldn't have signed for the part. I'll pick myself up presently. Let's try the last two minutes of the pas de deux again. I really muffed it the last time."

We rehearsed the steps several times until he was satisfied. Then we did the whole scene from the beginning and Theo called it a day. It was after four o'clock and we were ready to drop from exhaustion.

This time I was the first to leave the cabaret. But before I did so, I got Adeline's New York address from Theodoric, asking him to make two copies, one of which I gave to Oriano.

FOURTEEN

I was heading for the Volks when Steve's sports car drew up alongside me. "Hop in," he said. "It's cocktail time."

"I could use one," I said. "And a little talk."

"You look tired," he said.

"I am. Rehearsal didn't go too well until the end. But what I want to talk to you about is your aunt. I'm furious with her."

"Now what did she do?" As he spoke, he backed up the car, then shifted and headed for the road.

"I think I'd like a drink first. And a quiet ride to collect my thoughts. I'll tell you over cocktails."

"Fair enough. Believe it or not, I know a place where there's not a single slot machine."

"You mean it can stay open without one?" I asked, laughing.

"Come now, we're not that bad."

"I'm only joking," I said.

I slid down in the seat, let my head rest against the cushioned back, and closed my eyes, breathing deeply of the brisk, clean air, trying to relax. Not until the car stopped did I open my eyes. The exterior of the inn resembled a log cabin. Inside was a pleasant cocktail lounge. Beyond it, there was a dining room with red checkered tablecloths.

There was a quiet buzz of conversation, enough so that our discussion would not be overheard. I didn't doubt but that Amorita was well-known here, even though she had become more or less a recluse in her later years.

I told Steve, first of all, how I'd heard the putt-putt of the motorbike the night I'd been locked in the closet.

"Apparently, whoever gained entrance to the house was trapped in it until after you and Auntie retired."

I nodded. "Amorita and I searched the place when we thought we heard a prowler, but whoever it was could easily have hidden in her closet until after she went to sleep."

"Why do you say *her* closet?"

"Because I didn't go back to sleep. After I heard the sound of the motor, I got up and checked your aunt's room. She was in a deep sleep."

"It could have been Holly," he said.

"Or Oriano. Though I doubt that. He's been deeply depressed over Adeline's murder. He told me he was in love for the first time."

Steve looked skeptical. "Maybe, but knowing Oriano's reputation with the ladies, I doubt it."

"I don't," I said earnestly. "He sounded too sincere. But I want mostly to talk to you about your aunt."

"As I asked you before, what's she done now?"

I told him, beginning with the fact that she had attended the rehearsal on the previous day and had seen Adeline, then pretended she had not and asked for a description of the girl. I told him about his aunt's having had dinner with Theodoric, but making no mention of it to me."

Steve said hopefully, "She really doesn't have to inform you of her comings and goings, does she?"

"Not at all. But it seems to me it would be natural since you came to take me out to dinner."

He shrugged. "Natural, perhaps, but not necessary. Is that all?"

"Not quite. Last night after I retired, I heard the wheels of a car crunch along the driveway. I got up and went to the window. I could see two figures in the front seat of your aunt's car."

"Could you identify them?"

"No. But I checked your aunt's room and found she'd placed pillows in her bed to simulate a body."

He gave me a quick look. "That puzzles even me," he admitted.

"Me too. I was still awake when she returned and I heard the car, though I didn't hear her come upstairs. Only the sound of my doorknob turning made me aware of the fact that she was already in the house."

"Did she enter your room?"

I looked directly at him as I said, "When I saw the trick she'd played with the pillows, I locked my door when I returned to my room. She couldn't get in."

"Let's have dinner, then we'll take a run up."

"I'd like to drive the Volks up if you don't mind. I must have a car for tomorrow."

"Dinner first."

"I'm not particularly hungry."

"I'm the doctor, remember? I insist you eat."

He was right. I'd not eaten since I'd snatched a hasty breakfast at the Spindle. He told me then that Adeline had been strangled, probably with a scarf, before she'd been placed in the water. There was no water in her lungs and she'd been dead a few hours before her body was discovered. He added that she hadn't been sexually molested.

"You know, of course," he said, "that neither Holly nor Oriano has an alibi. Both claim they were driving from the time they left the cabaret until they returned to their rooms."

"Do you know when Oriano returned to where he's staying?"

"Not until ten. He was seen parking his car and going in. He was also seen when he went there in the afternoon to pick up his car. He went upstairs, changed to a dark blue suit with navy shirt and white tie, then went out to his car and drove off."

"Did he say whether or not he stopped anyplace?"

"He said he stopped no place. When he returned, he ordered dinner and had it sent to his room. It's already been verified."

We paused in our conversation while dinner was served. Steve and I had ordered chicken fricassee. With it were incredibly light dumplings which gave off a faint fragrance of rosemary. Whole carrots and slices of celery made it an appetizing dish. The hot rolls accompanying it were as light as a feather. Despite what I'd said about not being hungry, I didn't leave a morsel of food on my plate. Steve, thank goodness, did *not* say, "I told you so."

When we had both finished, I said, "I suppose you know that Holly now says she didn't fall in the lake."

He nodded. "She changed it once she knew Adeline was murdered."

"No," I contradicted. "Mirabel went to her room after we left the motel and Holly told her she took a spill. Perhaps she'd had time to think about it and decided to tell the truth."

Steve nodded. "Holly's lie—whichever story was a lie—isn't doing her any good."

"Oriano brushed her off, too. That hasn't helped."

"Why did he do that?"

"Because of the blowup yesterday when she protested to Mirabel about Adeline's getting the role."

"Holly hasn't done herself any good. Has someone else been selected for Adeline's part?"

I nodded. "Phyllis Grant. She's good."

We skipped coffee and left. Steve drove me back to the cabaret and I picked up the Volks, then followed him back to Castle Morvant. Halfway up the incline to the castle I groaned aloud, for coming toward us was the Rolls. Amorita, sitting stiffly erect, was at the wheel, but this time she was without a passenger. As she passed, she nodded briefly, but made no attempt to slow down.

Steve had slowed, as had I, but he accelerated and continued the climb. He drew up before the house and was out of his car and opening the door of the Volks for me.

"I'm sorry, Nicki," he said. "Your confrontation with my aunt will have to wait."

I nodded wearily. "It's just as well. I'm too tired for bickering."

"I can see you are. Why don't you have a nap? If I can get back later, I will. Just now, I'm going to see if I can catch up with Amorita, tail her, and find out what she's up to."

"I wish you luck," I said. "And thanks for being so understanding."

"No problem there," he said. "Sure you're not afraid here alone? I'll gladly wait 'til you pack and take you back to the motel."

"I'm not afraid," I assured him. I was really too exhausted to feel any emotion, except a warmth for the man standing before me. On impulse, I stood on tiptoe and kissed him. He was so surprised he could only manage a lopsided grin.

"Thanks, Steve, for your company and a delicious dinner."

"Thank you, beautiful," he said firmly. He escorted me to the door and unlocked it.

"You don't have a key, do you?" he asked.

"No," I replied.

"I'll see you get one." Then he returned the kiss. It was as brief as mine, but it made me feel better.

As I started up the stairs, I noticed a light at the far end of the drawing room. I wondered if Amorita had forgotten to extinguish it, or if she wanted it to remain on—or if an uninvited guest was abroad. I felt no fear as I descended the steps and approached the room. I was past that stage. Too much had happened. I could see now that the light was coming from behind a tapestry. Moving it aside revealed an open door. With a grim chill of apprehension, I looked around the room, then heaved a vast sigh of relief. The room was empty. It was a library, its shelves filled with books. On the large mahogany desk was a lighted lamp.

I noticed a blue folder lying open on the desk. Perhaps I'd have given no heed to it, except that on top of a sheaf of newspaper and magazine clippings was a newspaper headline bearing the name of Lorraine Brewster.

I slowly turned the swivel chair around, sat down, and bent over the folder, first determining that all of its contents dealt with the murder of the medium named Lorraine, on whose experiences our ballet had been based.

This was the initial newspaper account of her murder. It stressed the bizarre, included photographs of the house, the seance room, and even Lorraine's bedroom. Otherwise, there wasn't much in the way of background on the murder. She'd been found in the wooded area behind her home, dead from burns.

A clipping from the same newspaper of the following

day gave it more play and added other details, all of which I read in deep fascination. It seemed to me that I was reading about myself, because this was the girl I portrayed in the ballet.

It was stated that knife wounds were also found on her body, but that the fire was the primary cause of her death. She'd apparently been soaked in some inflammable fluid and set afire. I shuddered, but kept on reading.

The sensational case extended over several weeks and even important magazines were covering it. The cheaper crime magazines had a field day.

One of the better publications boxed and listed the chronology of the strange case, which set it all out for me in a manner both vivid and terrifying.

First, there was a so-called accident, when a heavy tree branch fell and almost killed Lorraine. To me, this was reminiscent of the sandbag which had almost killed me. Then a second accident was detailed. Lorraine, during some of her seances, would have herself locked in a small cabinet, her wrists and ankles tied, her mouth gagged so that she was incapable of movement outside the cabinet—and quite unable to make the sounds which she later claimed came directly from the ghosts she materialized. One time, the gag placed over her mouth had also covered her nose and she was almost smothered. That brought back the memories of my nearly smothering to death in the closet on the top floor of this very house. I couldn't stop reading, even though every word added to my terror.

One of the last items concerned a police detective who, searching Lorraine's house for clues, was almost killed when he was returning to his own home. Someone in a stolen car had tried to crash into his car at an extremely high rate of speed.

I was unaffected by that for the moment because, at the bottom of the pile of clips, was a thick envelope addressed to Amorita and bearing the return address of the Parapsychic Institute.

Within was a brief letter to Amorita. It stated that they were in receipt of one hundred dollars, and in return for this they were pleased to send her photostatic copies of the report Lorraine Brewster had submitted to their institute just prior to her death.

Apparently, the institute was an authentic and discriminating one, given to strong doubts about mediums and the ghosts they materialized, for it did not grant any measure of truth to Lorraine's report. I began to read it fearfully and intently, wishing I were somewhere else, surrounded by bright lights, many people, and something more than the eerie silence which filled this house. Had newspapers and magazines found this letter, the case would have been far more sensational.

The more I read, the more fearful I became, until I looked up, startled at the slightest creak. Some of the facts were already familiar to me, but reading them in this way, in the handwriting of the woman who made these claims and apparently was murdered because of them, brought me to a point of near-terror.

The letter wasn't long, but it was well detailed and there was not the slightest evidence that Lorraine was insincere about what she claimed to have undergone. She had apparently been an intelligent, well-educated woman, for there were no grammatical flaws in her writing, and she wrote vividly, with the intensity of one who did this writing while under a heavy mantle of fear. I leaned back in the chair, prepared to study this document carefully. I ignored the fact that this was private property and I had no right to be reading it—nor even to be in this room, which Amorita had so far not told me about. I was too engrossed in the letter to think of anything else.

FIFTEEN

The Directors of the
Parapsychic Institute
Trenton, New Jersey

Gentlemen:

Acting upon your request for a detailed account of what I profess has been a close contact with the spirit world, I am writing this description of what I have experienced.

It began last autumn when I was holding a routine seance for some paying clients. During the seance I felt myself slipping deeper into my trance than I'd ever gone before. I had to pull myself out of it because I was too frightened to continue, but during this episode a man was calling to me. Calling and calling, until I felt I couldn't disregard him any longer. It was with the most intensive effort that I aroused myself. I then went into an ordinary trance, wherein I became the medium through which my clients were able to reach their loved ones.

That night I couldn't shut out the memory of the deep trance. Because I believe in my ability to reach the other world, I conquered my fears and went deliberately, and alone, into a trance, seeking that deeper state. It came promptly. This time I seemed to awaken to find a handsome young man in the room with me. His garments were white and he appeared to glow. He reached out his hand for me and I moved toward him.

Let me explain that I am not a young woman, nor am I more than moderately attractive. Yet this handsome young man seemed captivated by me. He extended his arms as if to bring me to him. I found myself unable to resist. I got out of my chair and took several steps in his direction; then the whole room seemed to go into a mad whirl. There was a bedlam of strange discordant and ear-splitting sounds, and a great deal of confusion, but when the movement of the room and noise stopped, the young man was still standing there with the saddest of expressions on his face.

Standing between him and myself was a woman, also all in white. Except for a certain hardness to her features, she was quite lovely. But she seemed made of marble—heart and soul included. When I moved toward her, she fended me off with gestures that indicated I would die if I went to the young man.

He began to fade. The girl still remained vividly clear. Then, out of the shadows, came another girl, young and also lovely. She went straight to the one who had threatened me and I saw the older one's lips move as if speaking, but I heard no sound.

The first ghost, whom I now recognized as Katiana, a former ballet dancer, whispered to the young girl ghost. The latter moved up to the young man, whispered in his ear, smiled into his eyes, and beckoned to him to follow her. He did so, seeming quite captivated by her youth and beauty. This seemed to enrage Katiana, who made furious movements toward the other girl, who in turn seemed only to have been following orders. Katiana made threatening gestures and the other girl backed away, apparently terrified of the older ghost. Everything faded then and I awoke—not in the chair where I hold my seances, but outside the house, in my garden. I have no awareness of having gone there, but certainly I must have, for there was no one about who could have led me there.

These events so unnerved me that for three weeks I refused to go into a trance, but I needed money, my clients were insisting, so I returned to my profession. Everything went well and I began to relax. One night—it was September twelfth, I recall—my last client had gone. I had closed the door of my seance room for the night, but for some unexplainable reason, I returned to it and sat in my chair. At once I felt myself slipping into one of those deep trances.

This time the young man appeared again, standing close to me. As I arose, I was thrown violently back into the chair and Katiana stood before me. When I attempted to move, her ethereal forces held me fast. Once again the young man began to fade, a woeful expression on his face. I tried to go to him. Katiana screeched—this time she made sounds—and held me back. Once more the other girl appeared, again trying to intercede. Suddenly, Katiana made a savage attack upon the other and, just as suddenly, I found myself no longer in my home, but along the banks of a deep pond, located a quarter of a mile behind my home. The two ghosts were struggling. The one who tried to help me was suddenly hurled into the water. She vanished at once, while the first ghost faded slowly from my view.

That's all there is to it, except that I have a strange feeling that the young man will materialize once more and that I will try to go to him, for I seem unable to help myself. But Katiana will stop me. I know now that she claims the young man for herself and will not allow me to go to him. I am afraid that the next time he comes, I will die— perhaps in the same pond that swallowed up the ghost of the friendly girl. I do not understand any of this, but I have set it down as it happened and as I know the facts. I fear for my life, but I also realize there is nothing I, or anyone else, can do to save me.

I swear these statements are true. I know neither the significance of them, nor if they have any in regard to me, but I fear that I am going to be the next victim. I beg of you to consider this letter carefully and derive what you can from it, especially if I should meet with sudden death, as I fear I will. Perhaps there is some clue here by which you can find the proof of another world—one which exists all about us, but which so few of us can contact and so few believe in.

                    Sincerely,
                    Lorraine Brewster

I sat back, suddenly aware that I was bathed in perspiration. The full significance of Lorraine's letter struck me in all its horror.

Adeline, in the ballet, had represented the young ghost who distracted Oriano's attention, enticing him back to the nether world. She'd danced the role only once and had met her death by drowning . . . like the girl ghost in Lorraine's trance vision.

I checked the date of the letter to the Parapsychic Institute and that of Lorraine's tragic death by fire. More than a week had elapsed between her sending the letter and her death. I wondered if, in that time, anything else had happened. I reasoned that if it had, she might have reported this to the Institute. Certainly she'd given them a vivid report in the letter I'd just read.

I had taken the area code and phone number of the Institute off its letterhead and put through a call before I remembered the time difference. No business office in the East would be open at this hour. I was on the verge of hanging up when a man's voice greeted me.

I said, "Is this the Parapsychic Institute?"

"Yes, madam, it is. My name is Emery. I'm the secretary and if I may be of service to you. . . ."

"Thank you, Mr. Emery. I'm calling from Lake Tahoe and I forgot what time it is in the East. I know this is considerably after hours. . . ."

"We have frequent meetings. Tonight was one of them, and I'm here a bit later than usual. I take it this is a serious call? We get many that are not."

"It's quite serious. I have before me a letter . . . why, it's signed 'Malcolm Emery.'"

"Have I corresponded with you?" he asked with a good-natured chuckle.

"No. The letter is addressed to Amorita Davina."

"Ah, yes. About the Lorraine Brewster affair. Are you a friend of Miss Davina's?"

"Yes. I'm living with her and I'm calling from her home. My name is Nicolette Artaude. What I wish to know is whether or not Lorraine Brewster sent any further letters to your institute prior to her death. This letter is dated in September."

"Yes. We received one more from her."

"May I ask what information it contained?"

"Ordinarily," Emery said, "we do not give out such information, especially over the phone, but Miss Davina has been a steady and generous contributor to our institute. If you live with her, I take it she wishes the information as much as you do."

"She is very interested," I said. I didn't consider it a lie. She would be.

"Perhaps," he said, "you should hang up and let me call you back. I have Miss Davina's number. In that way, I'll know you really are associated with her. The call will be collect, of course."

"Please do," I entreated him. "I'll wait here."

I hung up. Three minutes later the phone rang and I was talking to Mr. Emery again.

"Please don't think I doubted you," he said, "but we must be as certain as possible that we're not dealing with crackpots, or with feature writers who constantly ridicule what we are doing. I also took time to get Lorraine Brewster's final letter from the files. Now, what did you wish to know?"

"If any further acts of violence were described in that letter."

"Let me see . . . I think there was something . . . yes. I'll give it to you in capsule form. She went into another trance—involuntarily. The young man appeared again, as did Katiana. This time there was no interference by any other spectral creature. The one young female ghost who had interfered had been driven into the pond by Katiana, even though she had apparently been summoned to lure the young man away from Lorraine."

"Yes," I said, holding my breath.

"It seems that this time the ghost of the young man took firmer action than he had before. He went to Lorraine and when Katiana intercepted him, he brushed her aside. Enraged, Katiana attacked him with a knife.

Just as Lorraine Brewster awakened from the trance, she heard a scream from somewhere outside the house. Miss Brewster thought it was a man's voice. She went out to search, but of course she found nothing."

Oriano was going to die! If the legend held true, if all the events proceeded on schedule, Oriano didn't have long to live. I steadied my nerves the best I could.

I said, "You seem to regard her story somewhat lightly, sir."

"Miss Artaude, the institute was founded to investigate all claims of the supernatural. We exist through donations, many of them from people who have been victimized by so-called mediums. Therefore, our purpose is to expose fakes and frauds and the methods they employ."

"But Lorraine died—mysteriously and horribly," I said.

"True, but we found nothing to indicate her death was supernatural. It was murder, without doubt, but the murderer was of this world. Undoubtedly a maniac."

"He must have been," I agreed. "I'm grateful for this information, and Miss Davina will be, too."

"Yes, Miss Davina was very interested in the story of Lorraine, believing it had supernatural aspects. That's why she wrote us, enclosing, I must say, a generous donation for a copy of Lorraine's letter."

"I know." I *didn't* know I could practice such deceit. "Thank you again, Mr. Emery."

"Not at all. We're at the service of anyone who thinks he or she is being duped by people who claim to contact the beyond. We have a standing offer of fifty thousand dollars to anyone who can prove contact was made. So far, no one has claimed it. No one ever will. Good-bye, Miss Artaude."

I hung up and attempted to digest the new information. What stood out most vividly in my mind were the violent sequences of Lorraine's story that had been duplicated with Adeline and me as the victims. Of course, the ballet was based on Lorraine's story. Yet I felt two attempts had already been made on my life. First, my almost being struck down by the sandbag, then my near brush with death in the sealed closet. But I'd been lucky—Adeline had been killed. In Lorraine's story, the final act was the destruction of the young man by the jealous Katiana.

Katiana had ordered the young girl to entice the male ghost away from the worldly Lorraine. When she'd done so, Katiana, in a fit of jealousy, destroyed her. When the young male ghost was still attracted to Lorraine, Katiana first destroyed him, then Lorraine.

That was not exactly the way Mirabel had written the ballet. She did not have Oriano destroyed by the jealous Katiana. I was to die, but not Oriano. He and Katiana ended the ballet together. Yet in the letter he was disposed of. I supposed Mirabel felt it would not be good box office to have him murdered, so she omitted that part of Lorraine's story.

Was my death by violence foreordained? I looked down at my hand, still on the phone which rested in its cradle. My knuckles were a stark white from the pressure I was exerting on the instrument. My temples were throbbing. I had a slight headache—brought on, no doubt, by tension and fear. Someone, or something, was trying to duplicate Lorraine's dreams, or what she called her trances.

"Look," I told myself firmly. "People who study the supernatural—the educated, intelligent and scientifically-bent individuals of the Parapsychic Institute—are unbelievers to the extent that they offer a fifty-thousand-dollar award to anyone who proves beyond doubt they have seen, spoken to, or materialized a ghost. There have been no takers."

The only other answer lay in a plot to destroy the ballet. But why? Amorita hated modern ballet—but it was absurd to think she'd kill people to keep the *Ballad of Lorraine* from being performed.

Yet she was an odd character. Perhaps there was a strain of jealousy involved. Because she was now too old to perform, did she envy those who could? I tried to imagine her homicidally jealous. Maybe. I just didn't know.

My agitated nerves were just beginning to calm down when a fresh thought occurred to me. A law officer sent to investigate Lorraine's home after her death had been almost killed by an unknown motorist while on his way back to headquarters.

Here, the law officer could be Steve Fenmore, the medical examiner. Yet if he was endangered, it certainly eliminated Amorita as a suspect. Who, then? But so far he'd not been threatened. . . . I suddenly realized that my career would have no meaning if anything happened to him. Which meant—I loved him and nothing must happen to him. *Nothing, nothing, nothing.* If the *Ballad of Lorraine* must be cancelled to prevent his being harmed, then it must be cancelled. Certainly, Mirabel would see the logic to that. Too much had already happened for her to dispute it.

Without further ado, I left the house, headed for the garage, and drove directly to the Spindle, hoping Mirabel would be there. I could have phoned, but I wanted a face-to-face confrontation. I could well imagine her distress when I told her what I felt should be done.

SIXTEEN

Mirabel, in orange-and-lime lounging pajamas, opened the door happily at my knock. She urged me over to the table where a graph of dancing steps was laid out.

"Theodoric gave me these this afternoon after rehearsal," she said. "He worked them out last night. The solo is for you. The pas de deux is for Oriano and Phyllis, who, incidentally, is even better than poor Adeline. How do you like your solo?"

"Anything Theodoric does is superb," I said, not giving the graphs a glance. "But at the moment, I have more on my mind."

She motioned me to a chair at one side of the table. She took the other and studied me intently.

"What's troubling you?"

"I don't want any part of the ballet."

"*What?*" She regarded me as if I'd suddenly lost my senses.

"I mean it," I said. "I just saw a file on Lorraine Brewster—the newspaper clippings. Also, I read a letter she wrote to the Parapsychic Institute. It upset me, so I called them. They revealed she wrote a second one. It was that one which made me decide to give up my role as prima ballerina."

She still looked puzzled. "Perhaps you'd better begin at the beginning. You don't make sense."

"It's simple. I don't want to be in the *Ballad of Lorraine*."

"Why not?"

"Too much has happened."

"I'll grant we've had mishaps since we came here, and what happened to Adeline has distressed everyone connected with the ballet. But don't walk out on me, Nicki. This is my big chance. I need you. I need help from everyone in the ballet. You know the choreography, your dancing and interpretation are beautiful. Don't let me down. I'm begging you, Nicki."

"I'm frightened, Mirabel."

She nodded understandingly. "I don't blame you. You had two mishaps, either of which could have resulted in your death."

"Both deliberate," I said. "Lorraine had two mishaps before her death."

"Surely you aren't suggesting that what happens in the ballet will happen to the characters in real life."

"Did you know that Lorraine, in the second of those trances, saw the young male ghost destroyed by Katiana?"

She smiled at my intensity. "I didn't know all that happened in her final trance. I think I can use that. I like it."

"I *don't* like it."

"I think it's Amorita who has you upset. I know how she detests the modern trends in ballet. Are you sure she isn't influencing you?"

"She isn't influencing me at all," I said. "She doesn't even know I'm aware of Lorraine's final letter to the institute. I doubt *she* knows of the existence of the letter."

"Just how did you learn of it?" Mirabel asked.

"I got the phone number of the Parapsychic Institute from the first letter. I found it on Amorita's desk in her library."

"I didn't know there was a library in the house."

"I didn't, either. I was attracted to a light in the drawing room. Upon investigation, I found that a tapestry concealed a partially open door."

"And Amorita," Mirabel said, "who was only too happy to discuss her interest in Lorraine with you."

"No," I said. "Amorita wasn't in the castle when I returned home. Besides, I was unaware that she made donations to the Parapsychic Institute, or that she was familiar with Lorraine's case."

"She told Theodoric and me—the day she invited us to the castle—that she knew little or nothing about the story of Lorraine. Apparently, that wasn't the truth."

"She's a strange woman."

"She certainly is," Mirabel replied slowly, emphasizing each word. "I think you should come back to the Spindle. She's exerting an influence on you of which you aren't even aware."

"That's ridiculous," I retorted. "She is evasive though. Or perhaps secretive is a better word."

"Just what is her interest in the Parapsychic Institute?"

"Do you know about it?"

"Yes, though I've had no contact with it."

"Amorita contributes to it."

Mirabel nodded but made no comment, and I continued. "She has a complete file on the case of Lorraine Brewster. I read where the police officer who was sent to Lorraine's home to investigate her death was almost killed on his way back to the station."

"How?"

"Another car attempted to collide with his. He swears it was done deliberately. He swerved to avoid the accident and crashed. He was uninjured, but his car was damaged to such an extent that he was unable to pursue the other car."

"It could have been a drunk driver," she mused.

"I didn't think of that," I admitted. "But I'm thinking of Steve Fenmore. He's the medical examiner and he questioned us regarding our whereabouts at the time of Adeline's death."

Mirabel said, "I believe he was your alibi." Her tone was light, almost teasing.

But I couldn't make light of it. "I'm worried about his safety. That's why I want to get out of the ballet."

"Oh, Nicki, *please* don't make trouble. You know you're under contract. Your reason for withdrawing from the ballet doesn't make sense."

"Why not?" I countered.

"You're not the sort to believe in ghosts."

"Right," I said angrily. "And I'm certain no ghost murdered Adeline, or cut the rope securing the sandbag, or locked me in a small, practically airtight storage closet."

"Isn't there anything I can say to bring you to your senses?" she asked, her tone pleading. "It's as if you're trying to destroy me. My reputation is going to be made or broken with the *Ballad of Lorraine*. I've worked my heart out on it. So has Theodoric."

"I know, and I'm sorry."

"So am I," she replied, once again in command of herself, "because I'm going to hold you to your contract. The company is assembled, a definite opening night is scheduled. I can't let down the people who are backing us. And I can't let you back out."

"You must. Holly is fully capable of taking my part."

"She's not as good as you. If she were, I might be reasonable. I suggest you go back to the castle, pack, and return here. If there's no room available, you may share mine until one is."

I stood up. "Why should I come back here when I'm withdrawing from the cast?"

"Because I'm asking you to." She arose and walked with me to the door. "It's because of this Steve Fenmore, isn't it?"

"Yes."

"You love him?"

I returned her direct look. "Very much."

She sighed. "Well, at least Holly will be happy."

I smiled. "I suppose Amorita will be, too."

"She'll be triumphant," Mirabel said coldly. "She's done a superb job on you. I may run up and congratulate her. I feel like slitting my throat. Everything I've worked so hard for is going down the drain."

"It will be a success without me. You wait and see."

"Go back to the castle and sleep on it," Mirabel urged.

"My mind is made up," I said. "Good night, Mirabel. Tell Holly she got the role without my breaking an arm or a leg."

"You broke my heart instead," Mirabel said as she closed the door softly behind me.

I walked slowly back to my car, telling myself I wasn't a quitter. I honestly felt someone wanted to stop the ballet from ever going on, even if he had to commit murder to do so. Perhaps what I'd done was cowardly, but I felt better now that I was no longer a part of the production. I knew I'd never get another role in a ballet, but somehow it didn't seem important. What did seem important was Steve's safety, and I felt that would be guaranteed only if I withdrew.

However, I couldn't help worrying about what might happen to the other members of the company. I'd been lucky. Not so Adeline. Would Phyllis' life be endangered now that she'd accepted the role? Not even Oriano was safe, now that Mirabel intended to change the ballet's ending. . . .

SEVENTEEN

When I entered Castle Morvant, I closed and bolted the door behind me. I noticed dim light drifting from the drawing room, and walked reluctantly toward the light. Glancing around the large, shadowy room, I saw no one. Relieved, I had started to turn—when I heard my name spoken. I pivoted slowly and my eyes searched the dark corners of the room.

"I'm in the library, Nicki." Only then did I catch a faint glimpse of light, visible beneath the tapestry. But not until I stood just inside the room did I realize why I hadn't seen it before.

The desk lamp wasn't lit. Only a fat, double-wick candle flickered on the desk. Behind it sat Amorita, elegant in a metallic hostess gown which gave off a silvery sheen. Her graceful hands rested on the desk atop the file of Lorraine Brewster. I'd left it open and hadn't bothered to rearrange the papers. It was closed now.

She said, "Are you angry with me?"

"I'm too upset to be angry with anyone, though I should be."

"Yes," she agreed quietly. "Please sit down."

"I'm tired, Amorita," I said. "Tired and frightened."

"Of me?" she asked.

"Do I have reason to be?" I countered.

"No. I'll admit I've played a little game with you. I've always had a sense of the dramatic. Melodramatic would be a better word."

"Murder is the word I'm concerned with."

"Surely you don't think I had anything to do with Adeline's death."

"I hope not," I said.

"I believe you'll find I couldn't have been involved," she said softly. "I was with Theodoric."

"You were also at the rehearsal when Mirabel selected Adeline to play the role of the young ghost, yet you pretended you had no idea of who she was. You let me go into detail describing the part she played and what she looked like."

She regarded her hands. "I admit that."

"Also, you left the castle last night and placed pillows in your bed to make it seem you were in it."

A trace of a smile touched her lips. "I take it you're a light sleeper."

"I wasn't sleeping. I heard the tires on the gravel and ran to the window. I saw your car head for the road. You seemed to have a passenger."

"Theodoric. He was using my rehearsal room to create new steps for the ballet." She smiled at my amazement.

I said, "I don't think it's funny."

"I suppose it isn't. I could say I don't have to account to you for my actions."

"Then there's no reason why you should have placed pillows in your bed to simulate your form."

"No reason at all," she agreed lightly, "except that, as I said, I enjoy playing little games."

"I haven't thought of you as senile," I said coldly.

"I haven't thought of myself that way." She was unruffled by my statement. "But perhaps I am. I have behaved childishly. However, I did not cut the rope securing the sandbag, I did not lock you in the storage closet in the attic, and I did not murder Adeline. I did not pretend there were marauders in this house your first night here. I honestly heard someone."

"There was someone," I told her. "I believe you returned before the person could get out, and he hid in the attic and remained there until we retired. You heard him attempting to escape. I think he hid in a closet in your room while you were downstairs."

"Have you forgotten Steve also searched the house before we retired?"

I had. "Perhaps there's a place in the attic he didn't think of checking."

She nodded agreement. "Are you too tired to go up there? We might find a place he missed where someone could conceal himself."

I was uncertain whether or not I was being lured up there again, but my curiosity outweighed my trepidation. She moistened the thumb and forefinger of each hand and snuffed out the wicks. I held the tapestry aside for her and we proceeded directly to the attic. She snapped on the switch at the foot of the stairs and we ascended and began to look around. The place wasn't cluttered and there were more trunks than furniture, attesting to Amorita's travels.

"Ah," she exclaimed, and pointed to a wardrobe barely visible behind stacked trunks. Steve might easily have missed it, or not even have realized that a person might have concealed himself in such a piece of furniture. We edged our way around the trunks to the wardrobe. It wasn't wide, but it was deep and certainly could conceal a good-sized person. Someone very tall would have to bend forward, but would not be too uncomfortable.

Amorita opened the door. I stepped inside. She said, "I'm going to close it. Tell me if you can see out."

Before I could protest, she closed the door. At the same time, the sound of the door knocker reverberated through the house. Amorita said, "Oh dear," and I heard her retreating footsteps.

I fumbled for a latch or knob to open the door from the inside, but there was nothing. I pushed on the door. It was solidly built; it didn't even rattle. I kicked on it and called Amorita's name over and over. I realized now that age must have affected her mind somewhat, to the extent that she could concentrate on only one thing at a time. When the door knocker sounded, her one thought was to go down and answer it. Or was she far more clever than she seemed?

I renewed my kicking and cries for help. How gullible I was. Certainly I should have been on guard. Instead, I'd stepped right inside without any urging from Amorita. I'd wanted to see if whoever had been here might have left a clue of some sort. Once I was inside, the opportunity was perfect for her to shut the door. I had no way of getting out. I placed the palms of my hands on the sides and tried to rock the wardrobe. If I could topple it over, it might splinter open. It didn't budge.

Then I heard the sound of a voice raised in anger, followed by approaching footsteps. I stopped and listened. I had begun to perspire profusely from the closeness of the place. I wiped perspiration from my brow with my hand, then once again pounded on the door with my fists and called out for help.

The knob turned and the door was pulled wide. I fell into Mirabel's arms. Her face was livid with anger. Amorita stood a distance away, her fingers pressed against her face, as if suddenly remembering that she'd shut me in there.

"I'm sorry, Nicki," she said. "My attention was distracted by the door knocker. Please forgive me."

I was still too shaken to speak.

Mirabel said, "Honey, for God's sake, pack your clothes and get out of here."

"Please." I moved free of her. "I want to go downstairs and sit for a while."

"I'll pack your clothes," she said. "I asked you earlier this evening to come back. I beg of you now to get out of here." She pointed a finger at Amorita. "This woman is insane. Her grandnephew should have her committed."

"I didn't mean to leave her up here," Amorita said plaintively. "Truly I didn't, Mirabel."

"I don't want to talk with you," Mirabel said, following me to the stairs. "You've upset this girl so much that she has withdrawn from the ballet."

"Oh no," Amorita exclaimed. "Oh, my dear Nicki, you mustn't. It's unprofessional of you to even contemplate such a thing."

"She's more than contemplated it," Mirabel retorted. "She's done it. Thanks to you."

I went directly to the drawing room and sat down in a big soft chair. I sighed with relief as I rested my head and closed my eyes. I heard both Amorita and Mirabel enter the room.

I said, "What I'm going to do is return to New York. I've had all I can stand."

"Perhaps we should all return to New York," Mirabel said disconsolately. "Of course, we'll have to rehearse without Oriano."

"That won't be good," I said.

"How well I know." Her voice mirrored her concern. "But we've no alternative. If Theodoric goes along with my suggestion and we leave here, you'll stay with us, won't you?"

"I'm afraid in the state I'm in, I couldn't do the role justice," I said.

Amorita said, "I disagree."

Mirabel smiled grimly. "I guess it's the only thing you and I agree on, Amorita."

"I'll admit that what I did to Nicki was shocking," Amorita said. "But truly, I'm upset too."

"By what?" Mirabel demanded.

"By all the things that have happened since you started rehearsing here," Amorita said. "They compare so closely to the trance Lorraine went into involuntarily."

Mirabel said, "At least you now admit you know the story of Lorraine."

"Yes," Amorita said, "I've always been interested in exposing mediums and the spirit bit."

"That's another thing we agree on," Mirabel said. "But you've frightened Nicki."

I opened my eyes. I was tired of the bickering of the two women. "No, she hasn't. The falling sandbag and being locked in the closet upstairs frightened me. But worst of all, Adeline's murder has made me believe that two others in the cast are slated for murder—plus a third who's not in the cast."

"Who are they?" Amorita asked.

"Oriano and Steve and me," I said.

Amorita paled. "Why Steve?"

"I feel he's the counterpart of the police officer who investigated Lorraine's death and was deliberately rammed by another car. What happened to the characters in Lorraine's trances seems to be happening to the performers playing those parts."

Amorita nodded. "Adeline played the role of the young ghost who entices Oriano away from Lorraine. In the trance, the young girl was forced into the pond by Katiana."

"How did you know the older ghost is supposed to be the ballet dancer Katiana, long dead?" Mirabel asked.

"Theodoric told me," Amorita replied, though I saw color suffuse her face.

Mirabel said, "You've been seeing quite a lot of him."

Amorita nodded. "Years ago, I helped him in his career. I was well established and he needed contacts."

"What's that got to do with your being together so much now?" Mirabel asked.

"We've done a lot of reminiscing," Amorita replied quietly. "He's been very kind. He even asked me to come to the rehearsal tomorrow and dance for the cast. I was pleased that he asked, though I have no intention of doing so."

"Why not?" I asked, much to my surprise. I had every reason to fear this woman, yet I couldn't, and I attributed this to Steve. I still felt that if she were dangerous, he'd have sensed it. I honestly believed she had become momentarily confused when the knocker sounded downstairs, and that this was why she had left me shut up in the closet while she answered the door.

Amorita looked pleased that I would address her. "It would be presumptuous of me."

"I think it would be a great treat for the cast," I insisted.

Even Mirabel seemed intrigued by the idea. "It would," she said.

"No," Amorita said, lowering her eyes. I knew she was pleased by our interest. I also sensed that she wanted to perform for us, but felt timid about it. It had been years since she'd performed before an audience of any kind.

"I'll make a deal with you," I said.

She eyed me speculatively. "What sort of a deal?"

"I'll play the role of Lorraine if you'll dance for the cast. Please, Amorita."

"You're not angry with me?" she asked. "Truly, Nicki, I didn't mean to shut you in the wardrobe."

"I believe you," I said. "Just say you'll dance for us tomorrow."

She came over to me and her fingertips lightly touched my cheek. "I'll dance, but not tomorrow. And you don't have to agree to play the role of Lorraine in exchange." She looked over at Mirabel. "You know why Nicki withdrew from the ballet?"

Mirabel sighed. "She came down and told me all about it."

I said, "Perhaps I have become too unnerved by what happened. I let my imagination run away with me."

Mirabel said, "I think that's a highly sensible explanation."

The low purr of a motor drew our attention. I recognized it as Steve's car and my spirits lifted when he entered the room. He embraced his aunt and greeted Mirabel and me. I stood up and went to his side.

He said, "Hi, beautiful."

I replied, "Hello, darling."

A half smile touched his lips. "Is that just a theater-type greeting?"

"No." I spoke with quiet assurance. "I love you and I'm saying it in front of witnesses."

Mirabel said, "Oh, God," and raised her eyes heavenward.

Amorita looked ecstatic. "At last, someone has snared my nephew."

Mirabel said flatly, "You gain a niece and I lose a prima ballerina."

"Not necessarily," Steve said. "If Nicki wants to continue her career, I'll certainly not object."

I smiled up at him. "I don't want to. Right now the idea of being a wife and mother seems very appealing. I wanted a nicely rounded family."

Amorita said, "I think this calls for a celebration. A glass of sherry to wish the couple happiness."

She went to a small bar, filled four glasses with the dark liquid, placed them on a tray, and brought them to us. As we sipped the wine, Steve kept one arm around my waist.

Amorita said, "I want to tell Steve about tonight."

"He'll have to do a lot of listening," Mirabel said.

He laughed. "A doctor becomes well practiced in that."

Amorita then related her interest in the exposing of mediums and of having been a heavy contributor to the Parapsychic Institute. She told of the file she had on Lorraine Brewster and of my seeing it. I continued the story, relating how I'd gone to Mirabel to tell her I was withdrawing from my role in the ballet because I feared the lives of two members of the cast were endangered. I explained that they had assumed the roles of the two in Lorraine's trance who were disposed of by a jealous female ghost.

Steve regarded me skeptically. "I'm afraid you've lost me."

I sighed. "I was afraid of that, but it's simple. Adeline was murdered the day she assumed the role of the young girl ghost in the ballet. Lorraine Brewster was murdered in real life and I play her in the ballet. Oriano is disposed of by the jealous Katiana in the play."

"And you think Oriano is slated for murder," Steve said.

I nodded. "Also, the police officer who investigated Lorraine's death was almost killed on his way back to the station."

Steve said, "I still don't get it."

I said, "You're the medical examiner here, and you were sent to examine Adeline. I feel that your life is also in danger."

"Oh, come *on*."

"I can't help it, Steve," I said. "I'm frightened for you, Oriano, and myself."

"I'm concerned about you," he said. "And if you feel you're in danger, I don't want you to have any part of the *Ballad of Lorraine*. But you don't believe there is anything supernatural about what has happened, do you?"

"Goodness, no," I exclaimed. "It's a human being, all right. But the pattern is there."

Mirabel said, "Nicki thinks the murderer is bent on doing away with those who are playing the characters disposed of in the story."

Amorita said tonelessly, "Everyone knows I dislike modern ballet and you may as well tell him, Nicki, that I shut you in a wardrobe in the attic a short time ago."

Steve regarded his aunt with annoyance. "What kind of game was that?"

Amorita sighed. "I'm getting old, I guess. I was distracted by the hammering of the door knocker and I went to see who it was. However, when I let Mirabel in and she asked where Nicki was, I recalled I'd shut the door of the wardrobe on her. We came up here immediately."

"I wasn't harmed," I said. "Steve, we believe that whoever locked me in the closet had to remain hidden because Amorita returned before he could escape. He was probably still here when you came. We went up to see if there was a possible hiding place."

"I searched the place, remember?" Steve said.

"We know you did," Amorita said. "But did you open the wardrobe in the attic?"

He shook his head negatively. "I didn't even see it."

Amorita said, "It's practically hidden behind stacked trunks, but I happen to know it's there."

"What about it?" he asked.

"I think he must have used the wardrobe. Anyway, Nicki stepped into it and I asked her to see if there were any peepholes in the door. I closed it on her just as Mirabel pounded on the front door. I got a little confused and went down to see who it was. There was no latch on the other side of the wardrobe door, and Nicki was trapped in there until Mirabel and I came up."

Steve said, "That was stupid."

Mirabel said, "Amorita told me what she'd done as soon as I came in. I ran up and got Nicki out."

"Incidentally, there were no peepholes, Amorita," I said.

Steve looked annoyed. "I think I'm going to take a little trip to the town where Lorraine Brewster held her seances. This is beginning to get to me, too. They might have gotten a lead on the murderer. What's the name of the place?"

"Hawthorne," I said.

"And I want to read the file, Auntie," he said.

Mirabel said, "I have to get back. Will you be at the rehearsal tomorrow, Nicki?"

"Yes."

"Good girl." She set down her empty glass, bade the others good night, and left.

Amorita stifled a yawn. "Please excuse me, both of you. I'm exhausted."

Steve studied my face. "So is Nicki. I'll take the file so she can get some sleep."

Amorita went into the library, returned with the large envelope, and gave it to Steve. She kissed him good night and turned to me. "My dear, I'm very happy about you and Steve. I only hope you'll be able to bear with me and my idiosyncrasies."

"I'm afraid I'll have to." I softened my words with a smile.

She kissed my brow and left the room. Steve tucked the file under his arm and we walked to the door.

"I'd like to stay," he said. "We have a lot of talking and getting acquainted to do—if we ever manage a few minutes alone. But now you need sleep. You're exhausted and I know being shut up in that damn wardrobe didn't help to calm your nerves."

"It didn't," I admitted, "but I'm over it."

He kissed me then, this time with fervor. When he released me, he said, "Are you positive—about us?"

"Absolutely," I assured him, and returned the kiss.

"You convinced me," he said, holding me close for a few moments. "See you tomorrow, and in the meantime, take care."

"I will," I assured him.

He opened the door and turned back momentarily to say, "Did I tell you I loved you?"

"No," I replied.

"I love you, Nicki."

"That makes it unanimous," I said. "Please step out so I can close the door."

He did, but not until he caught my chin in his hand and kissed me again. I slid the bolt on the door, put out the light in the drawing room, and went upstairs. I was tired, but exultant. I was in love and I was loved. What more could any woman want? I thrust all thoughts of fear and danger from my mind and was rewarded by a night of restful sleep.

EIGHTEEN

Though I overslept and knew I'd be late for rehearsal, I took the time to write a letter to Adeline's mother expressing my sympathy for her daughter's tragic end. Amorita came out of her room just as I left mine. She noticed the envelope in my hand and what she said next made her seem to be psychic.

"I informed Steve that I was assuming the expense of the coffin and transportation of Adeline's body."

"That's good of you," I held up the envelope. "I wrote to Adeline's mother."

"I will, also," she said. "I'm glad you're remaining in the ballet. You know that what you intended doing is unprofessional."

"I know," I said. "But my concern was for Steve and Oriano and—yes, myself."

"In view of what's happened, it's only natural," she said. "Who's taking Adeline's place?"

"Don't you know?"

She smiled self-consciously. "I deserve that, but I really don't."

"Her name is Phyllis Grant and she's good."

"She wouldn't be a part of Theodoric's corps de ballet if she weren't. Aren't you staying for breakfast?"

"Can't," I called back from halfway down the stairs. "I'll grab a snack at the coffee shop. I'm late now."

She called a good-bye, but I was out the door. I was familiar with the road by now and made good time. I dropped the envelope in the mail slot of the motel lobby and headed for the coffee shop, which was practically deserted. I downed my soft-boiled egg, juice and coffee, and went directly to the cabaret.

I entered the building to the strains of an almost full orchestra, a surprise provided by Theodoric.

"Why not?" he said when I questioned him about it. "The hotels around the lake all have orchestras. The men are happy to earn some extra money by helping us rehearse. They work only at night in the dining rooms and clubs. They may not be a symphony group, but they *are* musicians and they seem to be adapting to the score nicely."

"Wonderful," I said.

I noticed that Mirabel sat alone at one of the other tables, busily engaged in going over the libretto, frowning darkly at some of it, and I knew she was in the throes of revision. She looked up and beckoned to me.

"Good morning, Nicki. Sit down. I'd like your opinion on the second scene."

I seated myself and gave her my attention, careful not to reveal my distaste at what she had done.

"It will now be a complete tragedy, played exactly as Lorraine tells it in her second letter." She looked up and smiled. "I'm so glad you called the institute. After you left last night, I worked until almost dawn on it. Never once left my damn room. I called Theodoric and told him. Thought he was going to tear his hair out. Once I calmed him down, he started to choreograph. Look at it."

I studied the graphs and had to admit he'd done himself proud. "It's great. But what do you mean by saying you never left your room? You drove up to the castle."

She was making further notes and spoke without looking up. "A damn good thing I did. You'd be a dead prima ballerina if I hadn't. That Amorita." She shook her head. "Get ready, honey. Everyone's ready but you."

I started a leisurely walk to the dressing room, pausing briefly to extend greetings to some of the cast.

"Hurry, Nicki," Mirabel urged. "I want to go right into the scene and rehearse the movement of the dancers' luring you from the house. I want a perfectly cohesive formation."

I made my way to the dressing room. The top of Holly's dressing table was in order, giving no evidence of her being here. Then I remembered. She probably didn't have to put in an appearance if we were to work only on the scene in which the corps de ballet lures me from the house. A woolen fringed shawl was draped over Phyllis' chair, evidence that she was already on stage.

I returned to the stage just as Theodoric called for silence, then told us what he wished us to do. I seated myself in a duplicate of the chair which had been crushed. I was to be in the midst of a trance when the scene began. The lighting was dim, giving the setting an eerie effect.

The music began, the corps de ballet entered the house and danced around me. Slowly I arose and hesitantly followed their beckoning gestures. I stepped from the house just as Oriano, in white, materialized and came toward me. I raised arms and went to him. He circled me in a dance, first to observe me more closely. Satisfied, he moved in to touch my face, lift my hair, and let it fall through his fingers. Then slowly, almost imperceptibly, our feet began to move in unison and we moved into our pas de deux. His eyes adored me and I responded. My arms moved about his neck and we circled the stage in gay abandon. The corps de ballet were caught up in the spirit of our new-found love and danced around us. This scene was one of complete joy because Katiana, the jealous ghost, did not appear. The music had a lilting quality.

Oriano became bolder, attempting to lure me from the world of the living to his world of the dead. I responded by circling on pointe shoes. He lifted me as if to carry me away, but I leaped free of him. At that point, Phyllis entered the scene and the dance became a pas de trois.

The music, muted until now, began to grow in volume. The woodwinds increased the tempo and the strings hurried to catch up, until the music flooded the theater and the corps de ballet danced into the scene to join the festive, gay atmosphere. At the end of the scene, it was apparent that Oriano would have his way. Satisfied, he and his ghostly retinue faded. The lights dimmed, I re-entered the set depicting the seance room, and when the scene ended, I was in the chair, deep in the same trance. The set was the same as at the beginning of the scene.

Mirabel exclaimed happily at our performance. Theodoric, always the perfectionist, was more reserved in his praise.

"We'll move on to the third scene. Mostly a solo by Oriano. Now, Oriano, or do you wish to rest?"

"Now, please, while I feel the rhythm of the dance," he replied and took his place on stage. The orchestra, at a signal from its leader, started, and Oriano began his solo with the amazing grace and ease that had earned him the title of the best danseur noble to come forward in a decade. He held us spellbound, yet when the dance ended, he asked to do it again. This time he improvised some of the choreography and Theodoric nodded approval. He did what he was particularly good at—the bal penchés, the horizontal leaps, and the quick turns and spins.

Then Theodoric asked Phyllis and me to repeat our ballet de deux, after which he worked with the corps de ballet. We took a brief time out for a rest period and had a lunch of sandwiches and coffee, sent over from the coffee shop. We resumed our rehearsal and it was almost four thirty before Theodoric dismissed us.

I talked with Mirabel for a few minutes about a bit of business in the seance room, then I returned to the dressing room. I was still occupied with the ballet, concentrating on what Mirabel wished me to do, so my grasp of the dressing room doorknob was light and I turned it noiselessly. When I stepped into the room, Phyllis was standing before Holly's dressing table and I heard the soft click of the drawer. Her hands still rested on the outside of it and her face, reflected in the mirror, flamed in embarrassment. She resembled a child caught in the act of pilfering something.

"What are you doing at Holly's makeup table?" I demanded.

"N . . . nothing." She turned, but remained standing before the table, as if to prevent me from opening the drawer. There was open terror in her face.

I knew she couldn't have taken anything from it, for her hands were empty and she was still wearing her leotard, so there wasn't a chance of concealing anything on her person.

"What *did* I surprise you at?" I asked. "You look very guilty, you know."

She avoided my eyes as she spoke. "I just wondered what kind of makeup she used."

"I'm not that naive, Phyllis, nor are you. It's not a good idea to snoop around another's possessions. It's especially bad to do anything underhanded at present. It leaves you open to suspicion."

Her glance was hostile. "Are you accusing me of Adeline's murder?"

"I didn't mention Adeline," I said quietly. "What made you?"

"It's the way . . . I don't know." She took her coat-dress off a hanger and donned it. "I don't have to answer any questions you ask. If the police want to question me, they can."

"Didn't they already?" I moved up to Holly's table.

"Yes," she retorted. "I'm alibied."

Everything in the drawer seemed to be in order. I opened it wider and my attention was drawn to a silken piece of fabric twisted round and round. I thought it was a scarf Holly might have used to tie around her hair, yet there was something about it that didn't seem right. I picked it up. It apparently had been in water, twisted in just that way, and it had dried without being opened. I slid my fingers between the folds which seemed to want to stick together. It was badly wrinkled, but opened to a square. It was also water-stained. But what made me gasp aloud was a large initial in each of the four corners. The initial *A*.

I looked up, expecting Phyllis to be as shocked as I. She was gone. I glanced at the chair where her shawl had been tossed. It, too, was missing. She'd slipped from the room while my attention was diverted. Had she put the scarf in Holly's desk, or had it been here all the time? The drawer was paper-lined and dusty. There was no evidence that the scarf had been placed in here while wet, though that had no particular meaning. The question that came to my mind was, did Holly know about this bit of evidence?

I remembered now that Adeline had had it tied casually around her neck the last time I'd seen her alive. When her body was found, she'd not been wearing a scarf. But Steve had stated she'd been strangled before her body had been thrown into the water.

I twisted the scarf in the manner in which I'd first seen it, slipped it into my purse, changed to street shoes, and left the cabaret. A few of the cast left when I did and we exchanged farewells. I asked a male dancer if he'd seen Phyllis.

He replied that she'd left with the other girls, who were going directly back to the Spindle.

At the motel, I checked the number of Phyllis' room and went there. She answered my knock and paled when I asked to talk with her.

"Here or in the coffee shop," I said. "I could use a cup."

"No, thanks," she said. "Come in, Miss Artaude."

Though her manner wasn't friendly, it wasn't hostile, either. It was no time for subtlety or games, so I opened my purse and took the twisted scarf from it. She covered her mouth to stem her startled cry.

"What do you know about this?" I asked.

"Nothing."

"Then why are you afraid?"

She started to cry. "I had nothing to do with killing Adeline. The scarf was in Holly's drawer, not mine."

"If Holly murdered Adeline, she'd not be such a fool as to leave evidence like this around."

"Perhaps she didn't know what to do with it," Phyllis countered.

"She could have left it on the body," I said.

She was sobbing openly now. "I don't know anything about it. Honestly."

"Then why are you so upset?" I asked.

"Because . . . because I want to be in the ballet and if I'm suspected I'll lose the part."

"Why should you be suspected if the scarf was in Holly's drawer—and that's where I found it."

She stopped sobbing and regarded me with renewed fear . . . or was it guilt?

I said, "It wasn't in Holly's drawer. It was in yours. You transferred it to hers."

"I didn't." She started to sob again, uncontrollably.

"You did. You know you did. You took it from your drawer and put it in Holly's. It was a foolish thing to do"

"I didn't!" she screamed. "I swear I didn't!"

Someone in the next room banged on the wall for quiet. I knew Phyllis was lying, but I was getting nowhere. I'd give the scarf to Steve and tell him about it. He'd pass it on to the police.

"I said, "All right, Phyllis. You didn't put it in Holly's drawer. But remember, I saw you at Holly's makeup table when I entetred the dressing room. Your hands were pressed against the drawer as if you'd just closed it."

"You didn't see me close it," she exclaimed between sobs.

"No," I admitted. "But guilt was written all over your face. I'm giving it to the police."

"I don't care what you do with it," she retorted. Her sobs had lessened and as I walked to the door, the mirror backing it revealed the misery and fear which still consumed her.

I headed for the coffee shop. On the way I met Theodoric and invited him to join me.

"You be my guest, Nicki," he replied in his gallant manner. "I will buy you dinner."

"Thanks, Theodoric, but I have a dinner engagement with Steve—unless he has an emergency."

"With a doctor, one never knows." He patted my shoulder consolingly. "But he is worth waiting for, is he not?"

"He is," I replied with quiet emphasis. "The rehearsal went well today."

"Very," he agreed. He held up two fingers to the waitress. She nodded and brought our coffee.

"I missed Holly," I said.

"I gave her the day off," he said. "Amorita expressed a desire to get better acquainted with her."

"So that's why Amorita wouldn't dance for us today."

His eyes twinkled mischievously. "She asked me not to say anything to anyone when she asked me to invite Holly to visit her."

"Why not?"

He shrugged expressively. "One never questions Amorita."

"I guess one doesn't," I said. "I'm fond of her, but I don't understand her."

"Don't try to," he said. "But she has made a most generous gesture in regard to Adeline."

"I know. It was dear of her."

"Yes," he agreed, and added sadly, "The girl had a brilliant future. Only eighteen. Phyllis Grant is good. Did you know she is Mirabel's niece?"

"No!"

He smiled at my surprise. "Mirabel told me, but only after I had selected her. She said that Phyllis wanted to make it on her own. She'll never make it as a prima ballerina. Then again, maybe she will."

I was glad the conversation had shifted to Phyllis, for I was curious to learn more about her. Certainly the fact that she was Mirabel's niece was interesting.

Theodoric thought a moment. "Her face has a certain quality that a ballet dancer's face should have. I am a little old-fashioned when it comes to girls. I like them to have human qualities, but I want them to be ladies. I feel Phyllis has that quality, and I will say that Mirabel doesn't favor her."

I had to agree. More than once, Mirabel had spoken sharply to Phyllis when she wasn't interpreting the character as Mirabel felt it should be done.

"Are you headed back to Castle Morvant?" he asked.

"Yes. I want to rest awhile before I dress for the evening."

He nodded. "You worked hard today. I believe Amorita will dance for us tomorrow. You are in for a treat. She has already danced for me."

"I should think you two would argue constantly about classic versus contemporary ballet."

"We do. But don't let Amorita fool you. She loves contemporary ballet, but she loves a good argument better."

"So that's it," I said, yet I wondered if Amorita was playing another kind of game.

"She is also intrigued with mysticism."

"With the exposure of it," I corrected.

His eyes looked doubtful. "Maybe. I can't be sure. She's such a contradictory person, and she seems to believe in ghosts."

"But she's a heavy contributor to the Parapsychic Institute," I argued. "Their sole purpose is to expose mediums and frauds."

"That wouldn't bother Amorita that much." He snapped his fingers. "As I said, she's forever playing games."

"Well, I must run along. Thanks for the coffee."

"Thanks for your company, my dear."

I motioned for him to remain seated as I slid from the booth. I thought of stopping by to pay Holly a visit, wondering if I should show her the scarf which had been placed in the back of her dressing table drawer, but a glance at my watch revealed that there wasn't time. It was almost five.

However, I was in for a surprise when I drove past the front entrance of the castle on my way to the garage, for a motorbike was parked there. Oriano's—which Holly was still using. She must have been having quite a visit.

She and Amorita were in the hall when I entered.

"Hi, Nicki." To my surprise, Holly's greeting was actually warm.

"I'm glad you're still here, Holly," I said. "I discovered something today which I think you don't know about and should."

"What?"

I opened my purse and drew out Adeline's scarf. "Recognize it?"

"No. Should I?"

I opened it wide and held it up. The water stains were clearly visible from the light of the half-open door. Also, the initial A in each of the four corners. She regarded it soberly, and slow recognition dawned as to its meaning.

"Is that what Adeline was strangled with?"

"I believe so," I said.

"What are you doing with it?" Amorita asked.

"It was in Holly's dressing table drawer."

"You don't think I put it there, do you?" she exclaimed.

"No," I replied quietly.

"What made you look in my drawer?" she asked.

I disliked bringing Phyllis into this, but the story would have to be told anyway. I related how I'd entered the dressing room and saw her standing before Holly's makeup table, her hands on the drawer that she'd apparently just closed.

"Do you think she put it there?" Holly asked indignantly.

I said, "What I'm wondering is if she found it in her drawer, became frightened as she realized the significance of it, and transferred it to your drawer."

Holly's face colored with anger and she headed for the door. "Wait 'til I get my hands on her."

I caught her arm in a restraining gesture. "Don't do anything rash. She's Mirabel's niece."

"Great," Holly said flatly. "Where does that leave me?"

"A suspect, apparently," I said

159

"Even more so than before," she retorted, "since I don't have an alibi for when Adeline was murdered."

"You'll be questioned by the police," I said, "but so will Phyllis."

"What about you?" Amorita asked.

"I'll be in the clear. Phyllis admits seeing the scarf in Holly's drawer, but denies she put it there."

"Who could be doing this?" Holly exclaimed uneasily.

"If we knew," I said, "we'd all feel a lot better."

"And dance a lot better," she said.

Amorita, who'd been listening intently, said, "I think it's someone connected with the ballet. I wondered if it might be the combine that wants to purchase the property the cabaret is located on. I thought they might be playing rough, but they woudn't stoop to murder. I don't think they even had anything to do with cutting the sandbag rope. I neglected to tell Steve that I instructed my agent, even before the ballet came here, to proceed with selling the property. I happen to like what the combine is planning and I have no further objections to disposing of the land."

"What about Oriano?" Holly asked.

"What about him?" I couldn't see Oriano as a suspect.

She frowned. "I don't know. He has no alibi for the time of Adeline's murder, either."

"But what could be his motive?" Amorita asked. "He stands only to profit from the *Ballad of Lorraine*. It's an excellent vehicle for him."

Holly said, "I agree. But I happen to know he detests Mirabel."

"Why?" Amorita seemed fascinated at the prospect of Oriano's being a suspect

"I don't know," Holly said. "But I know he has no use for her. I could use a stronger word to describe his feelings toward her. Contempt—in capital letters. He makes fun of her and her clothes."

Both Amorita and I showed our surprise. She said,

"The police should know about that. Did you give them a hint, Holly?"

"I was mad enough at him to," she said with a reluctant smile. "But I didn't. I don't mind if you do, though. I prefer to remain silent. I'd like the use of his motorbike the rest of the time I'm here."

I smiled. "I'll tell Steve tonight."

"You'll have to, my dear," Amorita said, "because I must dress. I'm picking up Theodoric and we're going to take a drive. It's a beautiful night for it.

Holly left, and Amorita and I went upstairs. On our way, she said, "Holly is an interesting girl. Has a tremendous drive and will allow no one and nothing to stand in her way."

"That's good," I said, "except that because of her quarrel with Adeline, she's a prime suspect. And now with the scarf . . . well. . . ."

"I wonder if Phyllis also has that drive and figured she might inherit Adeline's part," Amorita mused.

"I don't want to think about it any more," I said. "I don't like everyone suspecting everyone else. It's unnerving."

"You're right, my dear." We headed for our rooms. "Take a warm bath and relax your muscles. Then dress and if there's time, rest."

"I will, Amorita. Have a pleasant evening."

"You, too."

NINETEEN

Steve arrived early enough to enable us to enjoy the sunset, spectacular at this time of the year. We found a quiet spot near Emerald Bay where we could also watch the tourist-laden cruisers making their swift runs around the lake, and where water-skiing schools were located, making the area alive with action. There was even a helicopter hovering above the lake.

"You can't say it's dull here," Steve observed.

"It's beautiful," I said. "I'm going to hate to leave."

"How much longer do you have?"

"Not long, I'm afraid. Rehearsals are going well."

"You may still see a change before you leave. If the snow comes early, and it often does, you'll find a whole new atmosphere. The few summer people here leave; the winter people come in with skis fastened to the tops of their cars. The bikinis vanish, the ski suits bloom, and I start setting broken bones."

He reached for the ignition key. It had grown quite dark and there was little to observe on the lake now. He said, "I've got a motorboat tied up at a marina close by and if I remember correctly, we should have a good moon in a little while. How about a cruise on the lake?"

"I'd love it," I said.

"Good." He reached for the radiophone. "I'll check in. Pray there are no calls."

There were none. We drove along the lake shore for about three miles, then he turned into a parking area near one of the smaller marinas. Moments later, he helped me aboard a sleek white-and-blue cruiser of respectable size.

Right on time, as if expecting us, the moon emerged from a clouded sky and the lake turned silvery and fantastically beautiful. I could even see the snow-topped ranges of the Sierras and the Carson Range. After a while, Steve cut the motor and we drifted. I curled up on a cushioned bench near the wheel and enjoyed the serenity.

"I'm going to Hawthorne day after tomorrow," he announced.

"Do you really think you'll learn something?" I asked.

"I hope so. That's where the story of Lorraine started. Perhaps there's an angle to it that Mirabel didn't know about. It might reveal the reason for what's happened here."

"Anyone could have read about it," I argued. "It was well detailed in the newspaper clippings Amorita kept."

"I wonder why she kept them?" he mused thoughtfully. "I didn't know it until she left that file where you found it, but I've seen other files since. She isn't lying."

"She's a heavy contributor to the Parapsychic Institute. Her interest in mediums is understandable—*if* it's for the purpose of exposing them."

"It is," Steve assured me. "Though it wasn't always."

"What do you mean?"

163

"My aunt was once engaged to marry a young man who was killed in the first world war. He was her only love. She told me, without the slightest trace of embarrassment, that she spent a great deal of money trying to contact him in the spirit world. She came upon a number of fakers who impressed her at first, until they were exposed. That's why she contacted this private organization that debunks spiritualism."

"Then it isn't just the Lorraine Brewster case that interests her."

"No," Steve said. "She showed me files she has on other unsolved mysteries that have nothing to do with mediums or mysticism. I talked with her at length today, because I was concerned after she shut you in the wardrobe last night. She was hurt because I questioned her so extensively, but what she did to you last night angered me and I told her so."

I smiled. "Thanks for your concern."

His arms enclosed me. "Why shouldn't I be concerned? I love you and I'm damned if I want anything to happen to you."

"I feel quite safe here."

He drew me closer. "I'd like to keep you here. And I want that murder solved. I mean Adeline's. Lorraine's, too, because I think that in some way they're connected."

"So do I," I said. "Unless that's what someone wants us to think."

"And is using the story of Lorraine, as it's incorporated in Mirabel's version, as a cover-up."

I slipped free of his embrace, opened my purse and brought out the scarf. "I almost forgot. This belonged to Adeline. I saw it on her the afternoon of the day she was murdered."

He snapped on the dashboard light. "It's water-soaked and quite wrinkled. Where did you find it?"

I told him in detail.

"Who's Phyllis Grant?" he asked.

"She's taking Adeline's place. I also learned that she's Mirabel's niece."

"What do you mean?"

"Theo didn't know she was Mirabel's niece until after he'd selected her to replace Adeline. Phyllis insisted she make it on her own. She will, too, but just now she's frightened—and with good reason."

"Does Holly know about this?"

I nodded. "She spent the day with your aunt."

He regarded me quizzically. "What do you mean?"

"Just what I said. I'm wondering if Amorita is trying to solve the murder in her own way. You just told me she has quite a file on unsolved mysteries. Why else would she bother with them unless she was attempting, in her own way, to solve them?"

"In all fairness," Steve said, "remember that my aunt is a sort of recluse. She's lonely, and that's as good a way as any to pass the time and keep her mind occupied."

"A rather macabre way, though."

"Yes," he agreed. "But it's *her* way."

"And to each his own."

"Right." He stuffed the scarf in his pocket. "I'll pass it on to the proper authorities. The cast will be questioned again. You too."

"Phyllis is the one they'll concentrate on, though. Obviously she's frightened that she'll lose her part."

"Not concerned about losing her life?"

"I don't think so."

"That's interesting. I wonder how many others in the corps de ballet would jump at the chance to play that role."

I laughed. "That's easy. Every single girl. You don't know the inner drive one must have in the entertainment world It's a jungle, and if one has to scratch and claw to make it, one will."

He regarded me soberly. "You, too?"

"If you'd asked me that before I realized your life might be in danger, I'd have answered yes. Fortunately, I've been lucky and never had to resort to chicanery, so I don't know if I ever really would. But now—since I've contracted to do the *Ballad of Lorraine*—I'm going to do it. When the run ends, I'll put away my ballet slippers and become a doctor's wife. That is, unless he'll be bored."

For an answer, Steve drew me close and kissed me. The embrace was long and fervent and when he released me, we were breathless. He reached for the ignition and started the motor.

"I'm taking you back," he said. "The combination of you in my arms and the moon is too much. I'm so happy that I feel drunk."

I laughed. "So do I. Mind if I slip my hand through your arm and sit a little closer?"

"I was hoping you'd do exactly that." We kissed again, but he kept his hands on the wheel. "I also hope the *Ballad of Lorraine* has a short run. We're too old for a long engagement."

I nodded and rested my head on his shoulder during the ride back. I forgot the fear and tragedy which had become part of the ballet, and thought only of life ahead with Steve. I'd be as dedicated to him as I had been to dancing.

TWENTY

The next day the entire cast was questioned by the police. Phyllis still denied she'd found the scarf in her drawer and transferred it to Holly's. Holly claimed complete ignorance regarding it. Theodoric looked deeply thoughtful during the questioning; Mirabel was quite agitated—as if the finding of the scarf had sounded the death knell for the ballet. Oriano, too, looked concerned; so much so, that I began to wonder. He'd told me he'd fallen in love with Adeline that day when they'd performed their pas de deux. Had he really, I wondered, or had he just said that to cast suspicion away from him? Holly was worried, but no more so than Phyllis. I feared Holly would take it out on the girl during rehearsal, but, in all fairness, she did not.

The rehearsal went well and Theodoric called a rest period, stating he had a surprise for us. I knew at once what it was. Amorita. He called the cast from the stage.

Chairs had been set up in rows and he motioned us to them. I was delighted to see Amorita wearing ballet slippers and standing at the rear of the house.

Theodoric went to her and led her to the stage. He instructed the orchestra, then told Oriano to accompany her. The music started up and the two of them, now on stage, began their dance. Mostly it was a solo by Amorita, with Oriano there in case he was needed. But he wasn't. Amorita performed as if she were decades younger. She was wearing blocked ballet slippers and stood en pointe without the slightest effort. She pirouetted gracefully and, while not as energetic as she once must have been, the practiced movements of her body were astounding. Oriano seemed flattered at being allowed to perform a pas de deux with her. She and he finished the dance and, as a finale, he lifted her and held her aloft. She remained motionless, her pose beautiful, as Oriano walked about the stage with her. Then, slowly, he lowered her, and her toes touched the stage, en pointe.

For a moment there was silence, then wild applause, with cries of approval from the cast. The musicians tapped their instruments or applauded by stamping their feet. It was the highest tribute they could pay to a performer, and Amorita gratefully blew them a kiss. Oriano whispered something in her ear, then raised her hand to his lips. Amorita kissed his cheek, spoke a few words to him, and he escorted her from the stage.

I went to Amorita, kissed her, and complimented her on her performance. She flushed with pleasure as other members of the cast gathered around her to praise her dancing. Finally, she left the group and came to me with the suggestion that we have a cocktail at the end of the rehearsal. I agreed, and she mentioned the name of one of the casinos nearby. Then she moved away from me and went to Oriano. They spoke quietly for a few minutes, after which she joined Theodoric and Mirabel at the table.

The rest of us went back on stage. We were now nearing the last quarter of the performance. We'd accomplished a great deal today and would soon be ready for a dress rehearsal. Our costumes had been sent out from New York. The only thing lacking was the scenery, but Theodoric had chalk-marked the stage, so we knew where the sets would be.

We had led up to one of the final scenes, a long one and a beautiful one. This was where Oriano, as the romantic male ghost, and Lorraine were to be married. When the vows were said, he would become mortal. That was Mirabel's latest innovation and it worked well. For the moment, the evil ghost portrayed by Holly had been vanquished. Phyllis had a good part in this scene, dancing joyously with a picked group from the corps in a number that was bound to draw favorable comment—and could well mean Phyllis' future as a ballerina. I was well satisfied with the way everything went, but I was, nevertheless, considerably surprised at Amorita's obvious interest. Theodoric had been right, apparently, when he told me she really liked contemporary ballet, but liked a good argument better.

Amorita and I left the cabaret as soon as the rehearsal ended and, each in our own car, met at the casino. The lounge was fairly full, and a babble of sound permeated the room. We sipped our cocktails quietly, content to look around and observe.

"I should have known better," Amorita said finally. "I found the *Ballad of Lorraine* fascinating. It tells such a complete and unusual story. It's happy and it's sad; quiet and exciting. It moves and holds the interest. While I will not deviate from my love for the classic ballet, the modern certainly has its place."

"I like the classics too, but times demand more than they offer. A repertory of both classic and modern is almost a necessity now, but I'm pleased you like the *Ballad of Lorraine*."

She smiled. "What I find most intriguing about it is the fact that Theodoric likes the book."

"Why shouldn't he?"

She made a graceful gesture with her hand. "He is quite intolerant about anything pertaining to ghosts and mediums."

"I didn't know."

"Yes. He was once a firm believer in the supernatural and he was convinced that his son, lost in World War II, had returned to him during a seance."

"And the medium was exposed?"

She nodded. "He asked the ghost of his son if his pet fox hound was with him in the beyond, and the son's voice not only answered that the dog was with him, but he supposedly had the dog bark. There was just one thing wrong with it. His son was afraid of dogs, having been, as a child, bitten by a large one. When the medium pulled that, Theo got up and walked out."

"It's understandable," I said. I finished my drink and excused myself. "Before Steve and I parted last night, he said he'd take me for a ride to Carson City and dinner if we got an early start. So I want to go back and change."

"Swann's Chalet. You'll love it," Amorita said. "I hope he takes you on the mountain road, it's spectacular. You may even get up as high as snow country."

"Don't mention snow," I chided. "Mirabel is terrified that we'll get snowed in here."

"You could, you know. Seems to me the summers grow shorter and the winters longer every year that I live. We've had heavy snow here before at this time of year. However, an early blanket of snow can catch the unwary and make things difficult, if you're not used to it."

I was passing through the lobby when I caught a glimpse of Oriano. He'd entered through another door and seemed headed for the cocktail lounge. I hesitated, was about to continue on my way, then stopped short and reversed my steps. I followed him at a discreet distance and watched as he entered the lounge, looked around, spotted Amorita, and headed for her table. He took her hand, kissed it lightly, and she touched his cheek in an affectionate gesture.

Puzzled, I moved away quickly lest she see me. There was no reason why she should have told me she was meeting Oriano here; but there was no reason why she shouldn't have. I wondered if she'd have been embarrassed had I delayed longer and had Oriano presented himself to her in my presence.

I walked thoughtfully to my car. Just when I felt that I finally understood the woman, I found myself more bewildered than ever by her. I headed back to the castle, and was no sooner bathed and dressed than Steve arrived.

He kissed me and admired my costume. I wore an ankle-length skirt of red wool with a matching silk blouse. Steve held my long, narrow, double-breasted Cuddlecoat and I slipped my arms into it.

"You look stunning," he said approvingly. "Let's get started."

"I'm hungry," I told him.

"We're headed for a chalet where we can have dinner served before a roaring fireplace."

"It sounds divinely romantic."

"You look divinely romantic," he said. "Hope you weren't waiting long."

"Not even a minute," I said. "We rehearsed long and diligently today. Your aunt danced for us. She's superb."

His smile showed that he was pleased. "Despite the little aggravations, I do love her."

"I can understand that," I said. "Perhaps one day I'll love her—once I comprehend her better. At present"—I shook my head in perplexity—"she bewilders me."

"What's she done now?"

"Nothing," I admitted. "She suggested we have a cocktail after rehearsal. We did. As I left the lounge, I saw Oriano enter the casino. He went directly to the lounge and sought her out. Apparently she'd been expecting him."

Steve nodded. "She plays her little games, but they're harmless. Now let's concentrate on us. In case you didn't know it, we've been climbing. We're above the snowline now. Watch when we take the next corner."

The car swept around it and Steve flicked on the high beams. I gasped in surprise and admiration, for in the blaze of those lights I saw the snow-covered pines.

"This snow will melt a couple of hours after the sun rises," he said. "It took a beating today, so there's not much left. You'll see the mountains by day, snow-covered and beautiful, before you leave. The weather bureau has issued a warning that there may be snow in the lower elevations in the next forty-eight hours."

"Will we be snowbound if it's heavy?" I asked. "The company is due to go back in a few days. We've done so well that Theo has decided we're all but ready, and we won't need Oriano in any rehearsals after this week. There'll be no reason for us to remain."

"That's the worst news I've heard in years," he said.

"For me, too. I'll miss you terribly."

"I have a little surprise for you. I've already made plans to take Amorita to New York for a couple of weeks when the theater season begins."

"How wonderful." I leaned over and kissed his cheek.

He grinned. "Feel the temperature changing again? We've been heading down for the last several minutes."

I did notice the difference. Presently I saw city lights, and soon we pulled into the parking area of a moderate-size redwood mountain inn called Swann's Chalet. Both food and service were excellent and the roaring fireplace lent an enchantment to the evening. Over cordials and coffee, Steve and I talked of our future plans, of our likes and dislikes regarding everything from food to people. We argued gently, respecting each other's opinions, even in matters of politics.

It was late when we started home, using the same winding, mountainous highway. We were silent during much of the ride, content in the full measure of the love we shared.

We'd reached the highest rise of the mountain chain, where I felt the cold again, but we were moving fast this time and it didn't last long. Halfway down the incline, it happened without the slightest warning

I saw at once that it was a pickup truck without lights. It must have been parked in a secluded turn-off, for it came out like a spider racing for its prey.

The right fender of the truck hit Steve's car broadside. Steve, wholly unprepared and relaxed, responded with the snap of a coiled spring. His grip on the wheel tightened, he turned sharply to avoid being bulldozed off the edge of the road, and he managed to crash his way past the truck.

I had been thrown against the dash, but I didn't think I was hurt beyond a few bruises. I had presence of mind enough to push down the automatic door locks so that we'd not be thrown out if a door buckled. Then I clung to whatever I could get a grip on.

The truck was after us before we'd cleared it by a dozen yards. From here on, the road was narrow, winding, dangerous, and unprotected on the ravine side. If we plunged off the road, we were going to crash and be killed.

Steve was an excellent driver; he knew mountain roads, but in that knowledge he was handicapped, for he realized that there was a maximum speed beyond which every added mile was like committing suicide. His car was built low and had great speed, but the driver of the truck, zooming down behind us, was not concerned with safety, only with killing us. His lights were on now, bathing us in their glare. I half turned in my seat to watch the truck.

"He's gaining," I shouted to Steve.

"If he keeps on, he'll kill himself—I hope," Steve answered. "Hang on. We'll get out of this."

The truck took the next sharp curve on two screeching wheels, while Steve had braked to make the turn in a far safer manner. The headlights were on top of us now, for Steve had slowed down while the truck had actually gained speed in its downhill rush.

"He's going to hit us!" I shouted.

"Hang on!" Steve said.

TWENTY-ONE

There was a crash as the truck rammed into our rear. For a few seconds, the light roadster rocked wildly, but its low silhouette gave it good stability and it settled down on four wheels again. The truck was behind us; a curve was coming up. Steve would slow, the truck would not, and as we rounded the curve, it would ram us again. This time it might be with enough force to throw us off the highway and the edge of the ravine.

We began to screech around the corner. For a few seconds, the truck was not in sight, though its headlights were vivid enough. I didn't know it at the time, but Steve was already planning a final and desperate move. The moment we were around the curve, he gave the wheel a twist to the left and the car shot off the road and into a shallow turn-off. There was no time to slow down very much, nor pace enough either, so the car slammed into the bank.

The pickup behind us started around the corner, rocked wildly, made the curve, and then, as if launched, shot off the side of the road. It seemed to me that it floated down, though that must have been an illusion. I buried my face in my hands and gave one convulsive sob. Steve's arms were around me.

"It's all right," he said. "We're safe."

I was trembling too violently to speak, but whether from relief or fear I didn't know.

Steve said, "I've got to go down there. Someone was in that truck. He must be dead, but I'm a doctor and I have to be certain. Also, I want to know who tried to kill us."

I got a grip on my nerves. "Let me go with you."

"Impossible. It'll be tough enough for me. I'll back out of here, make sure the car will run, and aim it downhill. If anything else happens, get away from here fast."

"I'll not leave without you."

He took a flashlight from the glove compartment. "If I flash it once, that means I'm coming up. If I flash it several times, that means the person in the truck is alive and I need an ambulance. Okay?"

"Yes . . . I'll see if I can find a phone. . . ."

"There's one under the dash," he reminded me. "Let's see if it works."

It didn't. The crash had knocked it out. The car, however, didn't seem damaged beyond the dents. Steve shed his coat, removed his tie, and then eased himself off the side of the road and on down the steep incline. He used the flashlight and it took him a surprisingly short time to reach the truck.

There was no difficulty in finding it because its lights were still on, though I expected it would be little more than a mass of smashed-up fenders and doors.

The flashlight kept winking, but the light was not aimed at me and therefore not a signal. The headlights of the truck went out. Steve must have turned them off. Then the flash was pointed my way and it winked only once. Whoever was in the truck didn't need any help.

I got out of the roadster and approached the edge of the cliff so that I might watch Steve's progress in climbing back to the road. I didn't feel any active fear now, only the residual kind that stays with one long after the terror is gone.

I heard a distant car motor and I looked up the mountain road. Far above, I could see faint lights, but they were going in the opposite direction. They only shone brightly because the car had swept around one of those sharp curves.

Steve crawled onto the road and leaned against the car, panting from the exertion of the climb. I waited anxiously, saw Steve shake his head from side to side.

"Nobody in the truck," he said. "No sign of anyone."

"Steve, there had to be someone driving it, and whoever it was must have been killed, or so badly hurt he couldn't move far from the wreck."

"I know. That's what I thought too, but if anybody is down there, he's well hidden. Or was thrown a great distance when the truck crashed. The truck belongs to a small delivery firm doing business at the lake. It was undoubtedly stolen."

I slipped back into the car. "I was right. They're trying to kill you. Just as it happened with a police officer when Lorraine was killed."

"Well, they didn't succeed," he said. "We're going back now and check on everybody who has a part in the ballet. My only explanation for what happened here is that the driver knew he couldn't manage the truck around that last bend, and braked to slow it down enough so that he could jump. It was a risky thing to do, but better than going off the edge. Whoever it was, he won't get back to the lake for a long time. If anybody is missing, he or she is going to have to do some tall explaining."

"Nothing passed us coming in the opposite direction. I'm sure of that."

"Yes, so am I. Why?"

"While you were down there, I saw the lights of a car going toward the top. If nothing passed us, the car must have been parked somewhere and we didn't see it."

Steve started the motor and we moved on down the mountain road. "If only the radiophone were working. I still think we can beat him back. There are a couple of other roads back, and though shorter, they're treacherous and winding. Nicki, thank you."

"For what?" I asked. "Your fine driving saved us. We'd have been rammed and pushed off the edge if you hadn't made the turn into the bank."

"If you'd panicked, I doubt I could have made it."

"Well, I panicked inside," I confessed. "I'm still churning. Oh, Steve, if we only knew what's behind this."

"We'd better find out fast. Maybe this time he went a little too far. In a couple of minutes we'll be off the mountain, and then I can make time."

We roared onto the road to the lake fifteen minutes later and at better than sixty miles per hour. We reached the lake and rolled to a stop in the parking area of the motel where the ballet troupe was staying.

We went into the lobby and called Holly's room. There was no answer. I glanced significantly at Steve, who put in a call to Theo's room. There was no response.

I tried Mirabel's room, and Steve called the casino where Oriano was staying. Neither of us got an answer.

Steve approached the desk clerk. "Did you see Mr. Coubet, Miss Rousseau, or Miss Larkin this evening?"

The clerk said, "They're all at the casino, waiting for you, Miss Artaude."

"But I didn't call them."

"Someone did. Left a message with me to inform the entire troupe to go to the cabaret immediately. It was a woman, and she identified herself as you."

"Was it muffled?" Steve asked.

The clerk thought a moment. "Maybe. Though I understood what she said."

Steve said, "Excuse me a moment." He hurried to a public phone booth. I knew whom he was calling. I could see him through the glass windows of the booth. His face was taut and tired-looking, but the muscles relaxed as he started to talk. He came out of the booth looking a great deal less worried.

"Amorita is at home. She says she didn't leave the castle this evening. I believe her. Whoever drove that truck had to jump. Amorita would have been killed."

I wondered, though I didn't comment. After seeing her dance this afternoon, I knew she was in far better trim than she seemed to be. But of course Steve was right. At her age, she could never have taken such a jump and not been hurt or killed. I felt she could be absolved of any suspicion. Besides, why would she wish to kill her nephew?

My heart was somewhat lighter as we drove to the cabaret—where the others were presumably waiting.

TWENTY-TWO

The entire cast, plus Mirabel and Theodoric, were in the cabaret. They'd drawn chairs together and formed a circle. The only light was a naked bulb of high intensity which gave their faces a drawn pallor. They regarded us with hostile eyes. They were both puzzled and indignant at having been roused from their beds and asked to come to the cabaret—only to find no one there.

Mirabel addressed me. "Why did you ask us to come here?"

"I didn't," I replied. "Steve and I went to the motel to see if everyone was accounted for."

Theodoric asked quietly, "For what purpose?"

"We were nearly killed tonight," I said. "Someone driving a pickup truck forced us off a mountain road."

Oriano said indignantly, "And you suspect one of us."

"I don't know whom to suspect," I said. "Any more

than I can account for someone's trying to murder us. But someone did try, just as someone did murder Adeline."

Steve took up the story. "The truck went off the road and crashed far below. There was no one in it when I reached it, and we found no trace of anyone below or on the road. We're here because the desk clerk said he received a call asking that the cast be awakened and told to come here at once."

Oriano said, "Someone called the hotel where I'm staying and left a message for me to come here when I finished my last show. It's not my idea of a joke."

"Nor is being run off the road, mine," Steve said. "But so long as you're all accounted for, there's no further need to keep you."

Mirabel said, "Thanks. Of course you know, Nicki, you have no business being out gallivanting. You put in a strenuous day's work and you need your rest. We're having a dress rehearsal tomorrow and I'm hoping everything will go smoothly."

"So do I," I said. Steve and I stood there watching them leave.

Theo said, "Please put the light out after you."

Steve nodded. The cast started to disperse. I regarded Holly, whose features were thoughtful, as if she were mulling over what we'd told her. Or did she know about it? Only Phyllis remained seated. Mirabel had started to go, but turned back when she realized Phyllis wasn't one of the group. The girl seemed in a high state of nervousness. Mirabel came back and rested her hand lightly on the girl's shoulder. Phyllis started at the contact.

Mirabel said, "Come on, honey." She turned to us. "The incident of the scarf has her very upset."

"Why should it?" I countered. "She only saw it in Holly's dressing table."

"Don't you believe her?" Mirabel asked.

181

"I don't know."

"I do." Mirabel spoke quietly, though I sensed anger in her tone. "She's fearful that what happened to Adeline might happen to her."

"I don't blame her for that," I said. "I'm frightened too. I've thought, from the first, that whoever killed Adeline is following the story of Lorraine's trances very closely. Lorraine was murdered too, remember. Which means I'm slated for the same fate."

"I know," Mirabel said. "And I'm beginning to have strong doubts as to whether or not we should continue the ballet."

"*You* are?" I asked, surprised. "I've had them for some time."

She sighed. "This is my big chance and someone seems determined to prevent me from ever getting this produced."

"Do you have the slightest suspicion of who that person might be?" Steve questioned.

"No," Mirabel said wearily. "If I did, I think I'd kill him."

I wondered if she had Oriano in mind. She urged Phyllis to her feet and led her to the door. The girl seemed to be almost in a trance. I'd never seen her look this way before. Certainly Adeline's murder was preying on her mind. It was preying on mine.

Steve and I walked to the door. He snapped the switch, plunging the interior into darkness. "The coffee shop is open at the Spindle. Let's have a cup."

I knew I should have had him bring me directly to the castle. Mirabel was right. I did need a good rest to do justice to my role during the dress rehearsal, but I felt he had a question or two on his mind and that this was his reason for suggesting the coffee.

The place was empty and the waitress brought our coffee immediately. Steve said, "Who knew we were going to Carson City?"

I smiled. "I told your aunt. That's all."

He frowned. "Somehow or other, Amorita seems to be playing a part in this."

"Yes." I gave him a direct answer because I couldn't help but think she was, in some way, connected with what had happened.

"I can't believe she'd be a party to murder." Steve insisted.

"Nor I," I said. "But her behavior is highly aggravating. I have a feeling she invited me to live with her so that she could stay on top of everything that's happening—and everything that's about to happen."

"Oh, come on," he derided. "She's not a snoop."

"I think she is," I countered. "This afternoon, for instance. Oriano showing up as I was leaving."

"What you're saying is that she may have told Oriano where we were going to have dinner?"

I nodded. I sensed his resentment of my attitude toward his aunt, but I couldn't help it.

"If she's in bed when we get back, I'm going to roust her out. We'll find out."

"Then let's go. I'm eager to know."

Steve pushed his untouched coffee aside and edged out of the booth.

Lights drifted through the windows of the first floor and Steve let us in with his key. He handed it to me, telling me to slip it in my purse, adding that he had a spare. We walked into the drawing room where Amorita, dressed in a lacy peignoir, was seated before a dying fire. With her was Theodoric, who arose, smiling at our surprise.

"I phoned the Spindle after you called me, Steve," Amorita said. "Theo wasn't there, so I left a message asking that he come up here when he returned."

"Why?" Steve demanded of his aunt.

"Because I sensed something was wrong when you

called me." Her eyes scolded him. "You hung up before I could get any further information from you. So I phoned my friend."

"All I know," Theodoric said, "is what Nicki and your nephew told us at the cabaret. But who summoned us, I cannot imagine."

"Nor I," I said.

"Did *you*, Auntie?" Steve asked.

"Certainly not," she exclaimed indignantly. "Surely you don't suspect me of the murder of Adeline Thornley."

"Everyone who had the slightest contact with the girl is under suspicion," Steve said.

"That eliminates me," Amorita said.

"It does not," Steve said. "You were at a rehearsal and saw Theodoric choose her. You watched her dance."

"Are you accusing me of snuffing out the life of a young girl who had everything to live for?" Amorita's voice was charged with emotion and there was a hint of tears in her eyes.

"No, Auntie." Steve went to her and took her in his arms. "Don't upset yourself. Nicki and I are tired. I know I've been rough on you. Forgive me?"

She nodded. "This has us all upset, and with good reason. You're all I have in the world. The thought of someone wanting to kill you and Nicki is unendurable."

"Did you tell anyone where I was taking Nicki for dinner?"

"Certainly not," she exclaimed indignantly. "Whom would I tell?"

"Oriano," he replied lightly.

She touched a hand to her brow. "I don't recall if I did."

"Think, Auntie," Steve pleaded.

"I'm trying to remember." Her serene brow furrowed. "No, I can't remember. We talked ballet. He complimented me on my performance today, and I told him that I wouldn't have been so sure of myself if he hadn't been my partner. How sure you must be of yourself with him, Nicki."

"Auntie," Steve pleaded, "never mind the dance. Did you tell Oriano where Nicki and I were going tonight?"

"I just don't know," she said. Then she brightened. "Oh, now I remember. Phyllis phoned you tonight, Nicki."

"Phoned me?" I asked.

"She wanted to speak to you. Said it was important. I told her if it was that important, she'd have to drive to Swann's Chalet, where you and Steve were dining."

"Phyllis," I exclaimed. "I can't believe she would do such a thing."

"She wouldn't." Amorita spoke with certainty. "Oriano invited her to be his guest this evening. He told me over cocktails. We discussed her dancing, also. He said—"

"Never mind," Steve broke in. "Did she say why she wanted to see Nicki?"

Amorita's smile was apologetic. "I didn't ask her."

Steve said wryly, "That isn't like you."

"Don't be rude, dear," Amorita chided.

Theodoric said, "I'm beginning to think Mirabel is right. Someone is doing everything—including murder—to prevent the *Ballad of Lorraine* from being performed in public."

"I'm going to Hawthorne tomorrow," Steve said, "to find out if there are any relatives of Lorraine's who resent what Mirabel has done."

"What has she done?" Amorita asked innocently.

"She has written a ballet of the trances Lorraine claims she had, and included Lorraine's tragic death," Steve said flatly. He addressed his aunt. "When you called Theodoric, couldn't you have left a message for him to call you?"

"I told you I wanted to find out what you were so upset about."

"Couldn't you have asked him over the phone?" Steve persisted.

"I was frightened, Steve. I wanted someone with me. All of a sudden even the familiar sounds in the house seemed threatening."

Steve's smile was one of resignation. "All right, Auntie. Just stop playing detective."

"Who said I was?" she asked indignantly.

"I'm saying it," Steve declared. "Isn't she, Theodoric?"

His look was noncommittal. "We were discussing the various members of the cast, but could think of no motive for the guilt of any one of them."

Steve turned to me. "Walk with me to the door."

There he said, "Be on guard. Watch Phyllis. Maybe she's the one who's caused all this trouble. Or maybe she learned something and wanted to tell you about it."

"Perhaps I should go back with you and see her," I said.

"I doubt it would do much good. She appeared tranquilized to me. Let her sleep on it. You need rest, too. Your face is tense."

"I'm wondering if you should go to Hawthorne."

"Why not?"

"You might be in danger there."

"I'll be on guard," he assured me. "Just make certain you are."

His kiss was gentle, and his whispered farewell was followed by his declaration of love. I moved to the stairs, hoping that Amorita wouldn't call me back. She didn't, and a glance into the room, from my vantage point on the stairway, revealed why. She was pouring sherry into two glasses. Theodoric looked quite content; Amorita looked serene. If Steve had upset her, she'd recovered quickly.

TWENTY-THREE

This was to be a dress rehearsal, but Theodoric wanted to run through the ballet once before we donned our costumes. It was he who suggested that the scene in which Phyllis attempted to flee from the avenging ghost should be lengthened. Mirabel wanted Oriano to attempt to save her from the wrath of Katiana, so that the dance scene would become a veritable chase, a fast-moving pas de trois until the end, when Holly would have her own way.

It was done three times and each time Phyllis faltered in her steps. The third time, Theodoric blew up.

"Take time out," he shouted. Rarely did he raise his voice, and then only when he was angry. He turned to Mirabel. "We must find someone else. Phyllis is wooden. I don't know what's happened to her."

"She's frightened," Mirabel said.

"She's supposed to be," Theodoric retorted. "But she's as stiff as a telephone pole."

"I mean," Mirabel said patiently, "because of what happened to Adeline."

"Then we'll have to replace her," Theodoric said.

"Oh God, no," Mirabel pleaded. "Not at this late date."

"I'll give her one more chance," he said. "All right, kids. We'll try it again."

I had no part in this, so I could sit quietly and observe the performers on stage. I, too, was dismayed by Phyllis' wooden portrayal of the young girl ghost. She'd done splendidly before. It was only today that her dancing revealed her inner turmoil. I wondered if it was guilt or fear.

I'd had no opportunity to speak to her, for when I had come in, Theodoric was showing her the graph which he'd made of the additional steps she would do in this number. I noticed that she was very subdued, but not as much as last night, when she scarcely seemed aware of what was being talked about. I recalled Steve's saying that she'd been tranquilized, and wondered if her quiet manner was the result. It might well be that her body couldn't respond as it should because of the drug she'd taken.

She seemed to brighten, and the pas de trois was moving to a climax—when she stumbled and fell flat on the stage. Oriano immediately went to assist her, but she'd gotten to her feet before he reached her; she burst into tears, and ran to the dressing room.

I heard Mirabel say, "Oh, my God. The poor kid."

I was already heading for the dressing room to see if I could calm her. Perhaps if she did know something, the burden of it was bearing down on her so much that she couldn't concentrate on the dance. I could hear her hysterical sobs through the door. I opened it and stood there, wondering if I should attempt to console her, or let her alone to cry it out. Ordinarily I would have, but I had to learn if there was something other than fear or nerves that prevented her from dancing as I knew she could.

I went to her and let my hand rest lightly on her shoulder. She cried out and jumped up from the makeup table. She backed away until she touched the wall and could retreat no further. I made no attempt to go to her.

"What's troubling you, Phyllis?" I asked softly.

"Please go away," she begged between sobs. "Please go away."

Mirabel came in then. "Phyllis dear, please. You're tearing yourself apart."

"I can't help it. I can't help it," she replied. Her face was distorted with anguish. "I'm frightened. I'm so frightened."

"Of what?" I asked. "Or whom?"

She turned her face to the wall and renewed her sobs. I turned to Mirabel. "Amorita told me that Phyllis called me last night."

Mirabel nodded. "I knew she was going to. She wanted you to practice with her last night."

"I thought. . . ." I was going to say that I thought her call might have concerned Adeline's murder, but I didn't bother to finish the sentence.

Mirabel said, "Theodoric postponed the rehearsal until later. I begged him to give Phyllis another chance. I'm going to take her back to the motel and insist she rest until then. She can't blow this opportunity any more than I can risk the *Ballad of Lorraine*'s never being produced."

I was already taking off my ballet slippers. I figured Theodoric would give Phyllis a chance to calm down. In one way I was glad of the delay. It would mean I'd have another day with Steve. In another way, I was irritated by it. It meant that Oriano, Phyllis, Steve, and

I were still at the mercy of whoever had murdered Adeline. Perhaps that was what had so unnerved Phyllis. If it was, it would be better if she retired from the role. There were other competent girls in the corps de ballet who could do as well. Still, it was sad that she had to fall apart. She wanted the part so much, and had been so happy when Theodoric had chosen her—then a completely different person from the depressed, hysterical girl she'd turned into.

Before I left the dressing room, I offered to accompany Mirabel and Phyllis. The former shook her head and motioned for me to leave. I nodded and closed the door quietly behind me.

Onstage I looked for Holly, but was told she'd already gone back to the motel. I drove there, for I wanted to talk with her. She was in her room, and when she opened the door at my knock, there was a guarded friendliness to her greeting.

She motioned me to a chair and took one opposite. "Phyllis really blew it, didn't she?"

I nodded. "I'm afraid Adeline's death was too much for her."

Holly shrugged. "She was glowing yesterday. I heard Oriano invite her to his show."

"Did she go?" I asked.

"How do I know? I wasn't there."

"Are you and Oriano still sulking?"

"Not exactly. We're friendly. I appreciate his letting me use the motorbike, though I'm careful not to take any more spills."

I smiled. "That's wise. Speaking of the motorbike, did you use it to return to Amorita's on the evening of the day that she invited you, Mirabel, Theodoric, and Oriano there?"

"No. Why would I?" Holly said coolly.

"Why would anyone?" I probed.

"Suppose you tell me."

"Okay, I will. I was locked in a fur storage closet in the attic the first night I was there. When I went there, the door was opened wide—I thought in a welcoming gesture. Lights were on all through the castle, even in the attic, but no sign of Amorita. I searched the house, including the attic, for Amorita, even calling out her name. When I went into the storage closet, lured there by a pile of furs on the floor, the door was slammed and locked. Then without my knowing it, it was unlocked. Whoever locked me in there, unlocked the door, freeing me."

Holly seemed impressed. "How do you know it wasn't Amorita?"

"Because after we retired, we heard someone in the house. We investigated and couldn't find anyone, but later I thought I heard the sound of a door closing. I got out of bed, went to the window, and saw a figure run toward the wooded area along the drive."

"A man or a woman?" Holly asked.

"I couldn't tell. Whoever it was wore a long cape and a wide-brimmed hat."

She said, "I wear a cape, but so do most of the girls in the ballet. Several of them have wide-brimmed hats, so what does that prove?"

"I heard a motor start up—it sounded exactly like the motorbike you use."

"Oriano's?"

"Yes."

"Are you accusing me of attempting to kill you with a sandbag, smother you in a closet and, failing that, murdering Adeline?"

"I'm asking you again if you went up to Amorita's that night on the motorbike."

She hesitated a few moments before answering. "No. Maybe Oriano did."

"Had he loaned you the motorbike that day?"

"Yes. He showed me how to ride it. I caught on

immediately, but I did not drive up to Amorita's. I won't deny that I would love the prima ballerina role in the ballet, but I wouldn't murder to get it. Also, Oriano could have taken the bike. I leave the key in it."

"I believe you."

"I'll bet." Her tone was derisive.

I stood up. "I'm not going to quarrel with you. I just wish Adeline's murder would be solved. We'd all feel a lot easier in our minds."

"I'll go along with that," Holly said. "I wish Phyllis hadn't fallen apart today. I want to get out of here. The cold seems to come right through the walls at night."

"We'll be out of here in a few days," I said.

Holly stood up and moved restlessly about the room. "I'd prefer it if it were a few hours. We're getting on one another's nerves, and we're all suspecting one another."

I couldn't argue that point. "Thanks for talking with me anyway."

She managed a smile. "I'm not a complete louse. And I didn't kill anyone."

"I believe you," I said, and I meant it.

"Thanks, Nicki." She walked to the door with me. "I hope Phyllis snaps out of it so we can have a dress rehearsal tomorrow. I can't wait to do Oriano in."

Under ordinary circumstances, I'd have joined her in laughter. But the memory of last night on that mountain road, when the truck bore down on Steve and me, was still fresh. So, too, was Phyllis' emotional outburst. I had the feeling she knew something. I could understand her being uneasy taking the role Adeline had; but hers seemed a case of stark terror. Of whom? Did she know the murderer? Or was it mere suspicion?

I was outside and on my way to the car, when I met Mirabel carrying two pieces of luggage. "No, I'm not leaving," she said. "These belong to Phyllis. I packed for her."

I was astounded. "You mean she's leaving the ballet?"

"No. She's just terrified to stay here. I'm checking her into the casino where Oriano's playing. It was his idea. He's offered to keep an eye on her. The sight of that scarf shattered her."

"Why should it?" I asked. "It wasn't even in her drawer. At least, she says it wasn't."

Mirabel made no reply. She opened the trunk of her rented car and deposited both bags in it.

"Or was it?"

She turned to me. "Honey, she's a sick girl. Let her alone. I want her in that ballet. It's her big chance. She's got as far as she did on her own. I don't want to see her muff it now."

"I don't either," I said. "But perhaps if she told the truth about the scarf, she could ease her conscience and concentrate on the ballet."

Mirabel looked pensive. "I tried to talk her into doing just that, but she won't."

"You mean she admitted the scarf was in her drawer?"

"Yes, but for God's sake, Nicki, don't say I mentioned it."

"Doesn't she realize she's under more suspicion now than she would be if she admitted the scarf was in her drawer in the first place? Only a fool would keep evidence like that around."

"I'll tell you this," Mirabel said, "but if you repeat it or pass it on to anyone, I'll deny it. Phyllis admitted to me the scarf was in the drawer of her makeup table. She panicked and put it in Holly's drawer. She'd just closed the drawer when you entered the room. She knew someone had placed it in her drawer. She suspected Holly and decided she'd put it back where she believed it came from in the first place."

"I can't believe Holly murdered Adeline," I said.

"Nor I," Mirabel said. "Holly is ambitious, but not that ambitious."

"Anyway, what would be the point of her doing that? Holly's role is far larger than Adeline's."

"True enough. But Oriano liked Adeline. In fact, I understand he fell in love with her."

I smiled. "With all respect to Oriano's talent, I think he has such a narcissus complex that he couldn't really fall in love with any woman."

"I agree. But he told Phyllis that Adeline was the first woman who made him forget himself. Poor Adeline's gone, so we'll never know if Oriano is being truthful, or just taking advantage of a tragic situation."

"Do you trust him to look after Phyllis?" I asked.

"No," she admitted. "But I don't think he'd harm her. He suggested this at the cabaret today. He felt that if she got away from here, she might be able to shut it out. She only has tonight. She couldn't sleep last night—said she kept seeing that damn scarf." Mirabel slammed shut the trunk of the car. "Oh God, who could have put that scarf in her drawer?"

"The murderer," I said quietly. "To cast suspicion on Phyllis. Or to frighten her."

"But why Phyllis?"

"Simple," I said. "Phyllis is dancing the role of the young girl ghost, who, in Lorraine's trance, was banished by being driven into the water. You've incorporated the same idea into the ballet. Adeline took the role first. She was strangled, then her body was tossed into the water. I take the part of Lorraine. Lorraine met death by fire. I meet with the same fate in the ballet. Oriano, after his marriage to Lorraine in which he is to become mortal—and I'm glad you incorporated that into the ballet—is destroyed by Katiana, the jealous ghost."

"What you're saying is that you're slated for death, and so is Oriano."

"And Steve."

"Why Steve?"

"Have you forgotten that the police officer sent to investigate Lorraine's death was driven off the road in his car by another car?"

"I had,". she said. "And you and Steve were driven off the road last night."

"If it hadn't been for his clever handling of the car, I wouldn't be standing here talking about it now."

She sighed. "I'll be glad when we get back to New York. I'll feel a hell of a lot safer in the concrete canyons than I do up here."

"I think I will, too." I headed for my car. "I hope Phyllis will be better tomorrow."

"Thanks, honey. So do I."

She waved a farewell and went back into the motel. I decided to pay Oriano a visit, and drove to the casino where he performed and where he had a room. But I was dissuaded in that, for I roamed the lobby and game rooms in vain, searching him out after calling his suite and getting no answer. There was nothing I could do now except return to the castle.

I wished Steve would return. Not that I had anything new to report, but I'd feel a lot better, knowing he was safe. I headed the car back to Castle Morvant, wondering if Amorita would be there.

I hoped Steve would return in time for us to spend the evening together. A quiet, pleasant evening before the fireplace at Amorita's. Romantic, enchanting, and wonderful.

TWENTY-FOUR

I'd no sooner reached the castle than snow began falling. I'd never seen such enormous flakes. It certainly would take no more than minutes before the ground would be covered, because the temperature had dipped suddenly and a strong wind had come up. I was glad to garage the car, and lost no time in getting inside.

Amorita looked pleasantly surprised to see me. "What happened?"

"Theodoric had to call off the rehearsal." I glanced out of the window at the now-heavy snowfall. "Mirabel's worst fear is coming true."

Amorita's smile was serene. "I just heard a weather report. It's not going to last."

Relief flooded through me. "That's good news. I don't like to think of Steve driving in this."

"If it gets too bad, they won't allow anyone to travel on the highways—not even with chains, which he has.

One keeps them handy up here." With that she dismissed the storm. "Why did Theo call off the rehearsal?"

"Phyllis had a bad case of nerves."

Amorita's brows raised thoughtfully. "Go upstairs and get into something warm. This place is drafty. I just took a roast chicken out of the oven. I baked some potatoes and there's carrot mousse. I'll have the gravy made by the time you come down."

"Were you expecting someone?"

"No. But at my age, you eat dinner at five or midday. It settles better on your stomach."

I donned a cashmere body stocking and over it wore a red wool knit pantsuit. My ankle boots were fleece-lined and felt quite comfortable. I already knew it was impossible to heat a place of this size in winter. I wondered how Amorita survived the season here. I asked her when I went downstairs.

She shrugged. "If it gets too bad, I go to Palm Springs. But I'm rugged, my dear."

"I believe it," I said.

"Now let's have our lunch while it's hot. I've lit the fireplace in the dining room and I've warmed our plates, but even with a fire, the room never gets really warm. The ceilings are too high."

The dining room was large, and gloomy even in midday. Amorita had two candelabras lit. The table silver and crystal gleamed, reflecting the candles' light. Although I felt no chill, neither did I feel as if I were dressed too warmly.

Amorita sat at the head of the table and I on her right. The room was long, with the fireplace at the far end. The logs snapped and crackled, giving off a cheery sound. After Amorita had served, she said, "Now tell me about Phyllis."

I well knew Amorita's overwhelming curiosity, and I felt she'd contained it well until she had the dinner on the table, so I lost no time in informing her of Phyllis' inability to perform.

Amorita said, "How very odd."

I complimented her on the food, asking, "Did you always cook?"

"Not until I retired and had lots of leisure, but I find it a challenge and am forever searching for new recipes. Sometimes I make up my own with not altogether pleasant results." She dismissed further talk of her cooking with an airy wave of her hand. "About Phyllis. What do you think upset her?"

"The scarf belonging to Adeline, which she found in her dressing table drawer and transferred to Holly's."

"So it came out that she did," Amorita mused.

"No, it didn't," I replied. "Mirabel told me. Phyllis confessed to her, but won't admit it to anyone for fear that she'll jeopardize her role in the ballet."

"She's done that anyway, hasn't she? I can't see Theodoric putting up with temperament, particularly with an unknown. The snow season's here and time is running out."

I nodded. "We were to have a dress rehearsal this morning."

"Theodoric told me. How does Mirabel feel about this?"

"She thinks Phyllis might get over her nerves if she gets away from the others. So Mirabel checked her into the hotel where Oriano is performing. It was his idea. He said he'd look after her."

Amorita sniffed. "Just *how* will he look after her?"

"I don't know, but apparently Mirabel is going along with it."

"Doesn't she know he's a rogue?"

"Everyone knows Oriano is a playboy," I said. "But perhaps in this instance, having witnessed Phyllis' emotional upset, he does feel a certain compassion for her."

"To Oriano, every girl is a conquest. Phyllis will be no exception."

"In this case, I can't agree. You haven't seen her. She's tragic."

"Why doesn't she ease her conscience by confessing to the police what she did?"

"I told you," I said, "she fears she'll lose her role in the ballet."

Amorita gave me a telling glance. "If I know Theodoric, she's lost it already."

"Mirabel will put up a fight for her niece."

"Why doesn't *she* go to the police and tell them what's troubling Phyllis? Certainly, finding the scarf in her dressing table drawer doesn't make her guilty of killing Adeline. The fact that the scarf was found in Holly's drawer doesn't make her guilty, either. Only a fool would keep evidence like that around. He might plant it elsewhere, but he'd certainly not want it in his possession."

My brows raised as a sudden thought occurred to me. "Do you suppose Holly could have put it in Phyllis' drawer?"

"I never thought of such a thing."

"Nor did I. Until this minute."

Amorita nodded at my plate, in approval. I'd eaten every morsel. She said, "I have a pudding for dessert."

"I couldn't," I protested. "I'm not used to eating so much at midday, and I gorged myself on everything. Just coffee."

"Fine. We'll have it before the fireplace in the drawing room."

We cleared the table, rinsed and stacked the dishes in the dishwasher, and carried the silver coffee service to the living room. The snow was still falling heavily.

Amorita poured and we sipped the strong beverage before the glowing fire. The logs were a good size and I asked her how she carted them in from outside.

"I don't," she replied. "I have a couple come here twice a week. They're very competent and look after me well. You've not met them yet because on the days they came, you were at rehearsal."

"I'm concerned about Steve driving here," I said. It was now impossible to see beyond the window. The flakes had the opaqueness of a blanket.

"Don't be," she replied serenely. "He's an excellent driver and takes no unnecessary risks."

"Nonetheless, I'll be relieved when I see him again."

"Why don't you go upstairs and rest for a few hours? I'm sure he'll be back by evening."

"I hope so," I said. "I feel uneasy about Phyllis, too."

"What do you mean?"

"I think she knows something."

Amorita regarded me with renewed interest. "About who might have placed the scarf in her drawer?"

"Not necessarily," I said. "It's just a hunch, but it's been nagging at me. I'd have talked with her at the motel, but I doubt it would have done any good. I tried to comfort her at the cabaret, but she was too hysterical."

Amorita looked regretful. "I never did get acquainted with that girl." She glanced out the window. "Unless the storm stops, I shan't today."

"I hope you wouldn't think of driving in this," I said. "I don't think the windshield wipers could handle those flakes."

"They couldn't." She took a final sip of her coffee and set the cup and saucer on the tray. "Will you have another cup?"

"No, thanks, Amorita," I said.

"Then go upstairs and lie down."

"Not until I help you straighten up."

She extended her arm and pointed an imperious forefinger in the direction of the stairway. "You'll do nothing but go upstairs and rest. You have circles under your eyes. You've been under too much of a strain, and you look it."

I knew it would be useless to argue with her. I thanked her for the delicious dinner and went to my room. I slipped off my pantsuit and lay on the bed, pulling the comforter over me. I really was fatigued, and it seemed that every muscle in my body ached. Not from overexertion, but from tension—something a ballet dancer should be free of. But I dropped off to sleep immediately from sheer exhaustion. When I awakened, a glance at my watch told me it was five o'clock.

I lay there only momentarily, for all the problems that had beset the cast since the day of our first rehearsal immediately filled my mind. I thought of Adeline's tragic death. Of Steve driving the treacherous mountain roads back. I thought of Phyllis, filled with agony and terror and a fear that she would lose her role in the ballet.

I washed my face, applied fresh makeup, put on my pantsuit, and went to the window. My spirits lifted when I saw that the snow had stopped altogether. The ground was covered, not deeply, but it would require careful driving. Though I'd driven in snow back east, I'd never driven in mountainous country.

I wanted to see Phyllis—to talk wih her. She might have calmed down once she got away from the motel and from the constant association with the other members of the ballet, who talked of nothing but what had happened to Adeline. It would unnerve anyone.

I went downstairs expecting to see Amorita, but there wasn't a sign of her. I returned to the second floor. The door to her room was ajar, but she was nowhere in evidence. I put on a jacket and left the castle. The stall next to where my Volks was parked was empty. It housed the Rolls and I knew then that Amorita's curiosity had gotten the better of her. Certainly she had courage to take the car out with the coating of snow on the ground just heavy enough to make driving treacherous.

I started out, maintaining a careful speed. I felt pleased with myself when I reached the south shore without even a minor skid. Of course, I'd checked the tires and found they had plenty of tread, but still I was relieved when I drove the car into the parking lot of the casino-hotel where Oriano was performing, and where I hoped Phyllis had been checked in by Mirabel. I angled the car into one of the slots, shut off the motor, and went inside.

At the desk, I asked if Phyllis Grant had been checked in. Assured she had been, I went to one of the house phones and asked for her. After several rings brought no answer, I hung up. She wasn't in—or wasn't answering the phone. I went back to the desk and asked for her room number, saying I'd just talked with her and been invited up, but had forgotten to ask her number. It was 514, on the fifth floor.

I entered the elevator and pushed number five. Oriano and I almost collided when I stepped off. He wore a silk robe over his costume, but seemed glad to see me.

"Going to catch the show?" he asked.

"I want to see Phyllis first," I told him.

Oriano gave me a wary look. "That girl's got problems."

"I know," I said. "I wish I could help her."

"I wish you'd get her out of my suite."

"Are you serious?" A more careful glance at his face revealed the stupidity of my question. His eyes held a worried look, and there was a nervous twitch at one corner of his mouth.

"She's drunk. I couldn't get rid of her. I'm late now. Please get her out of there, will you? I don't want any of that kind of publicity."

I knew Mirabel wouldn't either. Things were bad enough now. "Where is it?" I asked.

His finger darted out and pressed the hold button as the elevator started to close. "530-531."

At least I knew why she hadn't answered her phone. I was glad Theodoric didn't know her whereabouts. *Or Mirabel.*

I passed 514 and continued on to Oriano's suite, which was at the very end of the corridor. The door was closed, but I turned the knob. It opened. Phyllis, a glass in her hand, moved unsteadily about the room. She was wearing a flame-red peignoir over a matching nightgown. They were both ankle length and very beautiful. She'd have been beautiful too, except for her features, slack from alcohol.

"Hello, Phyllis," I said.

She turned, not fast, but like an automaton. Even so, she had to reach out and grasp onto the back of an overstuffed chair. She regarded me in silence and her head tilted to one side, as if she were having difficulty focusing her eyes.

"Well, well, if it isn't the prima ballerina." Her voice was slurred, her tone mocking.

"You should be resting," I said.

Her head lifted defiantly. "Make me."

"I wouldn't make you do anything," I said calmly. "I wouldn't even suggest you confess to transferring the scarf from your drawer to Holly's."

"I didn't do that," she retorted.

"You did. Mirabel told me."

"You're bluffing," she said. "She wouldn't. She swore she wouldn't."

"She told me only because she's worried about you."

Her laugh was strident. "Holly put the scarf in my drawer. I put it back in hers."

"How do you know?"

"I know. I know." She reeled over to the leather-padded bar and poured a generous amount of liquor into her empty glass. She reached into a thermos bucket for an ice cube and dropped it into the glass.

"Phyllis!"

I'd neglected to close Oriano's door, and was startled at the sound of Mirabel's voice. I turned just as she reached my side.

She addressed me, but her eyes were on Phyllis, who hadn't even turned. "I'm afraid I can't help her." Bitterness crept into her voice. "Oriano certainly hasn't. The louse. Where is he?"

"He went down for his show. He was late."

"Why did he let her drink?"

"He said he couldn't do anything with her and he asked me to get her out of here."

Her mouth was set in tense lines. "I didn't know she was in here. He's always thinking of himself."

I couldn't argue with that statement, but at least I'd never seen Oriano under the influence of liquor.

Mirabel said, "Please go, Nicki. I'll have better luck getting her back if there's no one else around."

"Sure I can't help?"

"Positive. I don't want any argument. With you here, she'll be difficult."

If Phyllis heard our conversation, she gave no evidence of it. She used the bar for support and devoted herself to emptying the contents of her glass.

I went downstairs, knowing I'd never get Phyllis to talk in her present condition. I didn't think I'd ever get to talk with her, for even Mirabel must know Phyllis couldn't perform tomorrow. She'd be in no condition to, and I knew Theodoric would accept no more delays or excuses.

I walked toward the dining room, where the music from the orchestra drifted out. Standing just inside were Amorita, Holly, and Theodoric.

I stepped to the rear of a double aisle of slot machines —where I had a view of the trio without their being able to see me. I saw Holly disengage herself from the group, head for the elevators, and disappear into one. Amorita and Theodoric were watching the performance.

They could easily observe it from where they stood. Amorita whispered something in Theodoric's ear and she, too, moved away toward the elevators.

I moved out from my place of concealment and crossed the lobby. I was just passing the elevators when one opened and Mirabel stepped out. She saw me and came to me at once.

"How's Phyllis?" I asked.

"In bed. Please don't let Theodoric know about her."

"You know she'll never be able to perform tomorrow."

"She will. She'll make it. I'll feed her lots of black coffee after she's had a few hours' rest."

I moved my head slowly from side to side. "You may as well accept it, Mirabel. Phyllis will never be in the *Ballad of Lorraine*. I think you'd help her if you convinced her that she should go to the police and admit she placed that scarf in Holly's drawer. The girl is sick with terror."

"She's convinced that Holly put the scarf in her drawer."

"Maybe she's right. But how will we know if she doesn't admit what she's done?"

"I can't reason with her," Mirabel said. She seemed on the verge of tears. "I'm at my wit's end. I feel as if I'm jinxed."

I didn't know if *she* was, but I now firmly believed that her ballet was, and I felt sorry for her.

She said, "I haven't even eaten today. After I checked Phyllis in here, I went back to the cabaret and looked at the costumes. They're beautiful."

"I'm sure they are. I'm looking forward to our dress rehearsal tomorrow."

"Pray to God we get no more snow."

"So long as Phyllis is resting, why don't you get yourself a snack?"

She nodded approval. "That's what I came down for."

I thought of Steve and wondered if he'd managed the

return trip. I dialed his number, got the answering service, and identified myself.

"Oh yes, Miss Artaude," the operator said. "Dr. Fenmore tried to get his aunt's residence. When there was no answer, he left a message for you. He's at Swann's Chalet. His car broke down and he's trying to get a ride back. He'll contact you as soon as he gets here."

"Thank you." I hung up, grateful for the message, but disappointed that Steve hadn't managed to make it back. But at least I knew he was safe. I was just hanging up, when I saw Theodoric standing some distance from the booth. He'd been observing me, but when our eyes met he turned and headed back to the dining room. I was tempted to follow, for I didn't like his furtive manner. Yet it could have been my imagination. He'd made no attempt to speak to me. Rather, he was watching me, as if wondering what I was up to— just as I was watching him. Suddenly I wanted to get away from here. I didn't know where I'd go, but I knew I didn't want to remain in the casino any longer.

I went outside and was heading for my car, when I heard some bystanders scream. They were pointing upward. I looked up at the front of the hotel and saw a body hurtling silently down, a flame-red nightgown and peignoir billowing back like a gaudy, ineffectual parachute. I pressed both my hands hard against my mouth as the body hit the marquee, bounced off, and struck the sidewalk with a terrible thud. I knew who it was, of course.

I ran over to where others had already formed a circle around the girl, and edged my way through them. Her blonde hair, bloodied now, almost covered her face which, miraculously, was untouched. Phyllis Grant.

TWENTY-FIVE

Her body had landed at the corner of the building. That was where Oriano's suite was located. Her room was not quite midway along the corridor. Had Phyllis returned to his suite after Mirabel came downstairs? I'd seen Holly and Amorita take the elevator—each at a different time. Where had they gone?

I entered the building just as they emerged from the elevator—together. I stepped outside and watched them head for the dining room. They entered it to the blaring music of the orchestra. Obviously, the news hadn't yet reached the entire hotel.

I went to a phone booth, deposited a coin, dialed Steve's number, and got his answering service. I asked the operator to call Swann's Chalet and leave a message for Dr. Fenmore that I was driving there to meet him. When I stepped out of the booth, quite a crowd had gathered in the lobby. Word of Phyllis' death had now traveled around.

Mirabel came inside, too stricken even to cry. "She must have gotten back to Oriano's suite."

I nodded. "May I help?"

"No, thanks. I'll do what's necessary. Just call the Spindle and tell Theodoric what happened."

"He's in the dining room, along with Amorita and Holly."

"You mean Amorita drove down here with the road this snow-covered?"

"Apparently," I said. "It wasn't too bad."

"You'd better take her back."

"I can't. I'm going after Steve."

"He can't help Phyllis." Then she nodded. "Oh, yes. He's the medical examiner."

"He isn't here," I said. At her puzzled look, I said, "He went to Hawthorne today. His car broke down on the way back."

She nodded absentmindedly. "Run along, dear. Nothing you can do here. I'll get Theodoric."

She headed for the dining room and I went to my car. It wasn't that I thought Steve wouldn't get a lift, but I just felt that I couldn't stay here any longer, and I feared going back to the castle. I wasn't usually superstitious, but it seemed as if this night were made for evil. Once in the car and on my way, though, I felt better. Driving steadied me. Snowplows had already been out and the road was cleared, though there were drifts of snow that one had to watch out for. I got careless once and the car spun halfway around. After that I was more cautious, slowing my speed to a point where I felt I had complete control of the car.

By the time I'd been driving for an hour, I reached the mountains. The snow had fallen more heavily here, but the plows had cleared the road. The snow was piled on the shoulders, though a wind had blown some of it back, making for treacherous spots.

The curves, particularly, were unsafe and I skidded off the road onto the shoulder. However, one rear and one front wheel remained on the road, giving me sufficient traction to free myself and continue. I felt that I must be no more than a half mile from Swann's Chalet, where I hoped Steve was awaiting me.

I was frightened. I was beginning to wonder if, in some way, Mirabel might have had a hand in what had happened. It didn't make too much sense, except that I couldn't understand why she'd left Phyllis alone in the room. The girl was incapable of knowing what she was doing. She was frightened—either of someone, or because of something she knew. And so she drank. I wondered if she had said something to Oriano. If so, why hadn't he told me?

Or could it be Oriano who was behind it? Did Phyllis fall from the terrace of his suite? Or was she murdered, as Adeline had been?

Then there was Amorita and Theodoric. They seemed to be together whenever possible. Was it friendship? Under ordinary circumstances, I'd have said yes, but the circumstances were *not* ordinary. Amorita had had an overwhelming curiosity regarding the members of the ballet since the day we'd arrived here. She'd invited the leading members of the cast, along with Mirabel and Theodoric, to her castle. She had sent Steve with a special invitation for me, while she'd awaited the return of the others at the Spindle.

She'd been secretive and deceptive on several occasions. Yet I couldn't believe that her liking for me was anything but genuine. I knew Theodoric's one love was the ballet. He lived for it and worked like one possessed, striving for perfection. I could see how utterly frustrated he'd been today when Phyllis could not go on with the rehearsal.

Then there was Holly. She was ambitious, selfish, and could bitch beautifully when the occasion warranted. Which it frequently did. But what motive could she have? This ballet was her big chance. She had disliked Adeline because Oriano's attention was drawn to the girl once she'd been selected from the group of dancers. He'd not be interested in a mere member of the corps de ballet. But if a girl were taken from there and given a larger part, it would be different. I wasn't convinced that he had fallen in love with Adeline. He'd use any incident for publicity purposes, in order to keep his name before the public.

I don't know how long I'd been traveling before I realized a car with one headlight was following me. At first I didn't give it too much thought, but then, as it neared me, I saw that it wasn't a car—but a motorbike. The driver was wearing a wide-brimmed hat, making identification impossible. Holly? Could it be? Of course. Who else? She had Oriano's motorbike. Was I to be her next victim?

Forgetful of the hazardous driving conditions, I stepped on the accelerator. I couldn't be more than a quarter of a mile from Swann's Chalet now. Perhaps not that far, but the road curved treacherously. The hill ahead was in my favor, for I could accelerate without fear of a skid. And I made it, though the motor was laboring near the top. There, directly ahead, the asphalt was slicked with snow, and I knew before I started the descent that I'd have difficulty. As I rounded the crest, the car went into a skid. I turned the wheel slowly in the opposite direction, but it didn't work. The car turned halfway and I started down, the front of the car facing uphill.

As it continued, the car turned slightly to face the side of the road. I prayed it would turn a little more, so that I'd once again be facing the direction in which I was headed. It did, but went into another skid which threw the vehicle off the road onto the shoulder. It hung precariously over the edge. Then I panicked.

I knew I'd never get the car out of this, and I couldn't remain here with the driver of the motorbike in pursuit of me. I got out of the car just as the motorbike crested the hill. It seemed to pause before it began the descent, and then moved forward cautiously, aware of my mishap and guarding against one of its own. Its headlights caught me in its glare, making me avert my head. I moved around to the front of the car. My headlights were still on and pointed the way downward to the bottom of the ravine. I had nowhere else to go. She could run me down on the road, or if she had a weapon, kill me.

I launched myself into space by stepping off the edge. I went sliding and slipping down along the deep snow until I was able to grab at a large bush and slow my descent. I stayed where I was, looking up at the road, wondering what Holly would do now. I no longer possessed the slightest doubt that it was she.

A flashlight beam suddenly swept down the incline. Before I could move, it crossed in front of me, came back, and I was vividly revealed. The light began to wobble, as if the person holding it was now sliding down the incline, too.

I let go of the bush, got to my feet, and reeled on down until I was at the bottom of the ravine. Behind me the light bobbed, coming closer and closer. She was following with an uncanny accuracy—or so I believed until I realized all she had to do was follow my tracks in the snow.

Despite my exertion, I was aware of the intense cold; but thanks to my warm garments, it didn't slow me down. Yet how could I go on like this? And where was I to go? There was no chance of getting any help. I'd lost all sense of direction.

Then I saw the stark outlines of the fire warden's

watchtower rising above the trees on the crest of the mountain top. If I could reach the tower and climb it, I might be safe, unless she had a gun. I had to gamble. There was no other refuge. I felt that if she were armed, she'd have fired at me before now.

I came to the foot of the tower. There was a stairway going up to the tower room. I ran up the several flights of stairs, slipping on the snow. I'd almost reached the top and was beginning to feel a sense of relief, when the flashlight caught me in its gleam. I groaned aloud. She knew where I was headed. I couldn't go down, and I knew she'd come up. I was trapped.

My hand reached out, felt for the doorknob, and I breathed a prayer, born of desperation lest the door be locked. It wasn't and I went inside, slamming it shut and leaning against it. At the same time, my fingers fumbled for the lock. My lungs labored from my exertion, but I turned and my fingers searched in darkness for a key. I located the lock, but no key. As my eyes became accustomed to the darkness, I made out a desk-like piece of furniture built against the wall. I presumed telescopes were placed here, or maps by which the fire wardens could coordinate distances and directions. I pulled open drawers in a frenzy of fear, knowing Holly must be nearing the tower, ready to climb the stairs.

I found a pack of matches. I lit one and held it high. Now I had a good look at this tower room. In a corner were long-handled shovels, used in fighting fires. One of these could make a weapon. I searched further and discovered several large cans of Sterno heat. I lit two. I'd warm my hands over their flames. But what really delighted me was finding a portable battery lamp. I lit it and placed it atop a chest. If anyone else was about, he'd see it. I prayed someone would. The tower was glass-enclosed, including the upper part of the door. Then I saw the key in a recessed niche alongside the door.

I ran to retrieve it and place it in the lock, but I

didn't quite make it. It wasn't just the face, glaring at me through the glass door, that petrified me. It was the madness revealed in it. And it wasn't Holly. It was Mirabel.

I threw my body against the door, but she was heavy and strong and flung the door open with such force that I was tossed across the room to land on the bunk bed. She slammed the door shut and leaned against it, breathing as heavily from her exertion as I had from mine.

She threw aside the wide-brimmed hat and flung off the cape which covered her. Over her shoulder was a zippered bag, fairly long and narrow. Certainly not a purse, but I couldn't imagine it containing a weapon of any sort. Her hands held none and looked blue with cold. I wondered why she went gloveless in this kind of weather.

Her smile was mirthless as she moved over to the table on which the Sterno cans, still flaming, sat. She held her hands over them, massaging them to restore circulation.

"So it was you who killed Adeline," I said unbelievingly. It didn't make sense. Mirabel destroying the ballet she had worked so long to create?

"It was," she said, not glancing my way, her attention still given to bringing feeling back into her hands. "And I had to push that stupid niece of mine off the terrace."

"You brought her back to Oriano's suite?"

"I did. Once I'd established an alibi."

"How did you manage that?" It was funny; I knew she planned to kill me, and yet I was genuinely curious. It occurred to me dimly that I might be in shock.

"I went down to the lobby and talked with you. In fact, you helped me by suggesting I get something to eat." She paused and looked over at me, madness gleaming from her eyes. "Of course, I put the idea into your head."

"I remember," I said conversationally. "And it was

213

you who loosened the boards on the stage, cut the sandbag, and shut me in the closet at Amorita's."

"Yes," she said. A shiver convulsed her. Only then did I notice that her pantsuit was lightweight. She must be frozen to the marrow. Perhaps she wouldn't attack me until her body heat returned. In the meantime, could I figure out a way to reach the door? Her ample form blocked my way.

"I've known how to ride a motorbike for a long time," she said. "Oriano did me a favor by letting Holly use it."

"And it was you who stole the light truck to run Steve and me off the road," I ventured.

"Who else?"

"But how did you get back? The truck was wrecked."

Her body was warming up now and she paused in her hand massage to make fists, place them on her hips, and throw back her head in a strange, harsh laughter. "Can't you figure it out? You've done pretty well so far."

I thought a moment. "Perhaps I can. You used Phyllis. That's why she was so terrified."

Mirabel's features tensed. "She chickened on me."

"Phyllis wasn't evil," I mused, pleased I could pretend a calmness I was far from feeling. "How did you convince her to help you?"

"I needed help in this God-forsaken country," she said. "Theodoric helped unwittingly by choosing Phyllis to take Adeline's place. I planted Adeline's scarf in my niece's drawer. She was terrified when she found it. She left the dressing room and told me about it. I suggested she place it in Holly's drawer, saying that you had placed it in hers."

"I?" She didn't make sense.

"I told Phyllis that you were in love with Steve."

"That's no lie," I said.

"It worked beautifully—or would have, if she hadn't gotten so scared."

"But why?"

"I told her you did it for his aunt, who hated contemporary ballet and was doing everything to destroy it. I said that it was Amorita who killed Adeline. Phyllis believed it. The night I followed you and Steve, she followed me in my rented car. She didn't know I'd stolen the truck—not until the investigation got under way. But when I covered myself and Phyllis by making the call to the motel, identifying myself as you and requesting the cast to assemble at the cabaret, she knew you were innocent."

I kept silent, trying to understand. Granted that she was insane, yet why would she destroy her own work? The *Ballad of Lorraine* meant everything to her. And she was its jinx, its . . . murderer.

Again, the room rocked with her laughter until I wanted to cover my face to shut it out.

"I thoroughly enjoyed it," she said. "I like playing cat and mouse. Even that night at Amorita's when I hid in the wardrobe and Steve came upstairs and searched the attic. Oh, yes—I unlocked the door of the fur storage closet when I heard Amorita return." She paused and her voice lowered in a confidential manner. "But you know, I almost gave myself away the time Amorita shut you in the wardrobe. I was smart enough not to close the door completely when I hid in it. I had no desire to smother to death. Steve never came near it. But when Amorita let me in that night and I asked where you were, she suddenly remembered she'd shut you in the wardrobe. I ran upstairs ahead of her and let you out. Anyone who didn't know of its whereabouts would never have located you."

I recalled the look on Amorita's face when Mirabel had let me out of the closet. She had both hands clasped over her mouth as if in dismay at what she'd done. Could it be she sensed then that Mirabel was the murderess? I thought of Mirabel's telling me only a few hours ago that Phyllis had fallen from Oriano's suite. How could she have been so certain, if she hadn't brought the girl back there? It wouldn't have been difficult. Phyllis was too drunk to protest.

"Holly will discover her motorbike is gone, and since you're missing, you'll be suspected. I heard you start it the night you slipped out of Amorita's after we had retired."

"I played quite a game of cat and mouse with the two of you."

"You hid in Amorita's closet and remained there until she went back to sleep."

"You're too smart," she said. Her voice was as cold as the night. "Much too smart to live."

"But it's true," I persisted. I had to keep her talking. It was my only hope of escape. My sole ally was time.

"No. I took the bike in the afternoon. Oriano and Holly made up. He took her for a ride. I doubt she's even missed it."

"But you'll be missed."

"I'll be far away from here. I can lose myself."

I nodded agreement. "And everything you worked so hard for through the years."

She took a step closer to me. "I killed Lorraine. She lied to me. She faked her trances. I believed in her."

"How do you know she faked her trances?"

"She told me Oriano loved me, that he would propose marriage. He should have. I got him the breaks."

"I'm sure you did. But he had the talent to go to the top."

She slammed the palms of her hands on the table, almost upsetting the Sterno cans. "He told me he loved me."

"He was ambitious, Mirabel. I imagine he's told that to a hundred girls and they all believed him. Did he really try to cultivate Phyllis?"

"No," she retorted. "It wasn't his idea to move her to

his hotel. It was mine. I had to get rid of her. I feared she was weakening. I knew you'd tried to get her to talk. I feared you, too. But I won't much longer."

I kept my tone quiet. "Are you really going to kill me?"

"You'll die as Lorraine did. In flames."

I managed to restrain a shudder. "Why did you write the *Ballad of Lorraine?*"

"Lorraine told me about her trances. I knew then that they were fakes and that she was a fake, but I thought what a hell of a good ballet it would make. And when I wrote it, it all became very real to me. But it *wasn't* real, you see, because *Lorraine* wasn't real. But *I* could make it real. I decided to dispose of the characters, just as Lorraine had disposed of them in her phony trances. I disposed of Lorraine. And I'll dispose of you the same way."

I tried bluffing her. "You know I don't believe you did any of the things you said you did."

"You better believe it."

She slipped the bag from her shoulder, unzipped it, and pulled out a soda water bottle containing a colorless liquid and stuffed with cloth. *A Molotov cocktail!* I jumped up.

"Stay where you are!" she exclaimed.

"I'm not going to stand here and let you throw that at me."

"If you move, I'll light it and throw it."

"You'll do it anyway," I retorted. The game was over. I was certain of it when she lowered the cloth to the Sterno flame, let it touch and ignite, and raised her arm to toss it at me. I screamed.

A voice called, "Mirabel!"

Startled, she turned so abruptly at the sound of another voice that she lost her balance and the bottle slipped from her hand. It dropped before her and exploded at her feet. She screamed with pain and fell as flames enclosed her.

It was Steve, followed by a state trooper, who entered the room. Steve pulled blankets from the cot and tried to smother the flames that consumed Mirabel. The trooper opened a drawer beneath the cot, pulled out two more blankets, and covered the burning floor with them. He stamped on the smoking blankets with his boots, then got an extinguisher and used it on Mirabel's covered form. Her cries had ceased.

Steve asked the trooper to take me outside. I was sick from what I'd witnessed. I turned back. Steve partially uncovered Mirabel. I hadn't noticed that he had his doctor's bag with him. He opened it, took a hypodermic needle from it, filled it, and injected it into her arm.

I turned away. Her face was hideously burned. I doubted she could be alive. Steve came out on the landing.

The trooper said, "I'll stay with her."

"No," Steve said. "I'm a doctor. I will. She can't possibly live. The hypodermic will keep her under until help arrives." He turned to me. "Lieutenant Carey will take you to the chalet. I'll see you there shortly. Thank God she didn't get you."

He kissed my cheek and went back into the tower room. I didn't know how he happened to be there, but explanations could wait. Lieutenant Carey guided me carefully down the stairs.

TWENTY-SIX

The following evening, Amorita, Steve, and I sat before her fireplace. He sipped brandy, Amorita and I chose sherry. Mirabel had died without regaining consciousness.

Steve said, "I learned that Mirabel grew up in the town of Hawthorne. She and her sister were raised by an aunt who was a stern disciplinarian. Mirabel never knew love or kindness, and though she had a sister who married, the sister didn't bother with Mirabel until her own daughter expressed an interest in ballet and was discovered to be quite talented.

"I suppose Mirabel was getting even with her sister by using Phyllis?"

"No doubt of it," Steve said. "I talked with Mirabel's sister. She said that Mirabel had always been a chronic liar, had had a violent temper and, on occasion, drank. But she could also be a very likeable woman."

I said, "Remember the night she came up here and opened the door to the wardrobe, releasing me?"

Steve and Amorita both nodded. Amorita said, "That was when I first suspected she had a hand in what was happening at the ballet."

"Why?" Steve asked.

I smiled, but let Amorita tell it. "Mirabel went directly to the wardrobe, which you couldn't even see unless you knew it was there."

I said to her, "I recall the expression on your face when I stepped out of the wardrobe. I remembered it last night."

Amorita's features expressed self-reproach. "I should have voiced my suspicion to Steve. I did to Theodoric. He ridiculed me."

"It's understandable," I said. "Theodoric worked closely with Mirabel. Obviously, she never displayed any of those characteristics."

"She was two people," Steve said.

"A split personality?" I asked.

"I'm afraid so," he said. "The evil side took over finally. The *Ballad of Lorraine* became very real to her and she was determined to dispose of the characters."

"She told me." I shuddered. "I didn't exactly understand . . . I guess I see it a little bit. She didn't have a chance to dispose of Oriano."

Steve said, "She got her niece drunk and sent her to Oriano's suite. You spoiled it by putting in an appearance. She had to bring the girl back to her room and alibi herself."

"Which she did," I said, "with my help."

Amorita said, "A good thing I called Steve's answering service. When the girl told me you'd gone after him, Nicki, I lost no time calling the chalet."

Steve said, "Fortunately, it was just at the time when a state trooper was trying to get me a ride back. We left at once in search of you and spotted that light in the tower."

"How did you know I was in danger?" I asked Amorita.

"While you were still napping, I took the car and went to the Spindle to talk with Theodoric about Phyllis. As you know, I'm a mystery buff. Also, I had a personal interest and concern for you, Nicki. You're not a coward. But I could see how distraught and worried you were about Phyllis when you returned yesterday. I pleaded with Theodoric to go to the police and tell them about her. I told him that if he didn't go, I would. I also told him that Oriano had talked with me about Mirabel."

My brows raised in curiosity. "Did he tell you she was infatuated with him?"

Amorita gave an impatient shake of her head. "He admitted quite freely he used Mirabel to make contacts. That he encouraged her to think he cared about her. It's pathetic when you think about it. Then, when he'd met those people who observed him dance and were impressed by his talent, she wanted him to marry her. He laughed at her and ridiculed her love for him."

"Mirabel's sickness wasn't helped by those around her," I mused.

"Anyway," Amorita went on, "that was when Theodoric started to worry. He feared other members of the ballet might be in danger if the murderer was Mirabel, and he was beginning to give credence to the fact that she was guilty. We were just leaving to talk with Oriano and ask that he tell the police what he'd told us, when Holly met us in the lobby. She was fuming. The motorbike was gone, and she had been invited by Oriano to go over to the casino. We brought her with us."

I colored with embarrassment. "I saw the three of you and stayed out of sight, but watched you. Please forgive me, but I wondered what you were up to."

Amorita said, "Theodoric and I talked with Holly in great detail. She swore she had told the truth when she'd said that she passed Mirabel in her car, heading for the Spindle, the night Adeline's body was found."

Steve nodded. "Mirabel had probably seen Adeline

221

heading for the lake and followed her. She invited the girl for a ride and Adeline, so grateful for the part she'd just been given, didn't want to refuse."

I said, "Mirabel must have strangled her in the car, removed the scarf, and at a secluded spot dumped her in the water."

Amorita said, "When Holly, Theo, and I reached the casino, Holly expressed a desire to talk with Phyllis, hoping she might get her to reveal why she was so unnerved. I wasn't certain I could trust the girl and decided to see for myself. We met in Phyllis' room, but of course, she wasn't there. Mirabel had brought her back to Oriano's."

"And pushed her over the terrace," I said.

"Was that hard for Oriano to take?" Steve asked.

Amorita sniffed contemptuously. "It *was*, last night. Today, with the papers filled with the story, he's reaping a million dollars' worth of publicity. And that, for Oriano, is manna from heaven." She suppressed a yawn and stood up. "Well, my dear, it's my bedtime. I hope you'll forgive an old woman her snooping."

I reached out and grasped her hand. "I'm grateful for it. If you hadn't shown such concern, I wouldn't be curled up here, being warmed by the fire."

She eyed us with affection. "Or by the loving glances my grandnephew is giving you. I think it's time I retired and gave you two a little time to yourselves."

"We'd like that." Steve arose and kissed his aunt. "Then we want to discuss our forthcoming marriage."

"Will it be soon?" she asked.

"That's up to Nicki," he said. "But as I told her, we're too old for long engagements."

"He's right, Amorita," I said.

Amorita bent down and kissed my cheek. After she left, I arose and went into Steve's arms. The danger and fear were over, and the future held great promise.

FOR SUPERIOR, SPELLBINDING
SUSPENSE, READ THE MASTERFUL
GOTHIC NOVELS OF

Dorothy Daniels

from WARNER BOOKS

THE BEAUMONT TRADITION (86-254, $1.25)
THE CALDWELL SHADOW (88-560, $1.50)
HILLS OF FIRE (75-867, 95¢)
JADE GREEN (86-192, $1.25)
THE LARRABEE HEIRESS (88-586, $1.50)
A MIRROR OF SHADOWS (89-327, $1.95)
THE TORMENTED (86-284, $1.25)
THE APOLLO FOUNTAIN (84-800, $1.75)
DARK ISLAND (84-801, $1.75)
DIABLO MANOR (84-802, $1.75)
THE DUNCAN DYNASTY (84-803, $1.75)
THE HOUSE OF BROKEN DOLLS (84-804, $1.75)
THE HOUSE OF MANY DOORS (84-805, $1.75)
THE LANIER RIDDLE (84-806, $1.75)
THE MARBLE HILLS (84-807, $1.75)
SHADOWS FROM THE PAST (84-808, $1.75)
THE SUMMER HOUSE (84-809, $1.75)

THE BEST OF THE BESTSELLERS FROM WARNER BOOKS!

DAUGHTERS OF THE WILD COUNTRY (82-583, $2.25)
by Aola Vandergriff
THE DAUGHTERS OF THE SOUTHWIND travel northward to the wild country of Russian Alaska, where nature is raw, men are rough, and love, when it comes, shines like a gold nugget in the cold Alaskan waters. A lusty sequel to a giant bestseller.

THE FRENCH ATLANTIC AFFAIR (81-562, $2.50)
by Ernest Lehman
In mid-ocean, the S.S. Marseille is taken over! The conspirators —174 of them—are unidentifiable among the other passengers. Unless a ransom of 35 million dollars in gold is paid within 48 hours, the ship and everyone on it will be blown skyhigh!

DARE TO LOVE by Jennifer Wilde (81-826, $2.50)
Who dared to love Elena Lopez? Who was willing to risk reputation and wealth to win the Spanish dancer who was the scandal of Europe? Kings, princes, great composers and writers . . . the famous and wealthy men of the 19th century vied for her affection, fought duels for her.

THE OTHER SIDE OF THE MOUNTAIN:
PART 2 by E.G. Valens (82-463, $2.25)
Part 2 of the inspirational story of a young Olympic contender's courageous climb from paralysis and total helplessness to a useful life and meaningful marriage. An NBC-TV movie and serialized in **Family Circle** magazine.

A Warner Communications Company

Please send me the books I have checked.

Enclose check or money order only, no cash please. Plus 50¢ per copy to cover postage and handling. N.Y. State residents add applicable sales tax.

Please allow 2 weeks for delivery.

WARNER BOOKS
P.O. Box 690
New York, N.Y. 10019

Name ....
Address ....
City .... State .... Zip ....
_____ Please send me your free mail order catalog